THE FLORENTINE PURSUIT

A SEAN WYATT THRILLER

ERNEST DEMPSEY

138 PUBLISHING

Copyright © 2024 by Ernest Dempsey

All rights reserved.

No part of this book may be reproduced in any form or by any electronic or mechanical means, including information storage and retrieval systems, without written permission from the author, except for the use of brief quotations in a book review.

All names, places, and events are either fictional or used in a fictional way. Any association to these real or imagined is purely coincidence.

PROLOGUE
FUNCHAL, PORTUGAL | 1921

"He is here, Your Majesty." The servant bowed low, his tattered black jacket swinging behind his knees. The garments were far removed from their once-stately appearance. Worn and unkempt, the clothes reflected the once-proud station he served—and its fall.

"You are a loyal friend, Johannes," Karl replied. "But you no longer need to bow before me. I am not the emperor anymore." He looked around the hotel lobby with subtle disdain. "I sit on no throne. Only a sofa anyone with money can enjoy. And it wouldn't take much of that."

"You are my emperor, Your Majesty. That will never change until the day I die."

Karl inclined his head and gave a regal, appreciative nod to the man. "Thank you, Johannes. Please, send in our guest. I am most curious to hear what they have to offer."

"At once, Your Majesty."

Johannes spun around and walked back toward the front entrance of the hotel, passing an international assortment of guards along the way.

The hotel was luxurious enough for most people, but for a man who'd been a member of the powerful Hapsburg Dynasty, Karl saw it for what it truly was—a glorified prison.

The crimson tapestries, the mosaic tiles on the floor, even the plants growing in the corners seemed to mock him as he sat on the sofa, his arms stretched out across the back as he waited for his guest to enter the room.

None of the guards seemed to pay him any mind, though Karl knew if he tried anything suspicious, they would snap into action.

He'd been here for the last several months, and nearly lost track of time more than once. The island was far away from his native Austria and the seat his family had occupied for so long.

Of all the wars, conflicts, and political battles his family had faced through the centuries, it had been Karl who failed in the the most devastating way possible. He wore that like a cloak weighed down by anchors on both shoulders. The once-proud posture he'd always carried had been replaced by the droop of defeat.

A cough snuck up on him from deep within his chest, and he doubled over, leaning between his knees until the fit had passed.

The coughing had become more frequent these last few days. Karl blamed the climate on the island of Madeira for being too humid. The reality was his body was quitting on him, and he knew it.

Karl didn't let on to anyone else except his personal physician—a useless old drunk who could only prescribe liquor and rest to ease the sickness.

What the former emperor wanted was to go somewhere warmer, dryer—Morocco perhaps, or the sands of Tunisia. Anywhere along the North African coast would do. The dry air and hot air would clean him out, but Karl knew that would only last so long.

His body was reflecting the stress, and the utter devastation he felt, as a result of being the one to lose everything his ancestors had built for generations.

The truth was he didn't want to live anymore. Not like this. He and his family were little better than commoners, and prisoners of those who had defeated him and his allies in the Great War.

He sat up straight again, breathing easier for a moment but knowing that the fits would return again at some point.

The guards at the doors stepped back as Johannes entered once more, this time followed by a man in a bowler hat and a matching black suit with white shirt. His black tie disappeared behind a black vest covering his abdomen. His mustache was wide like thick cat whiskers, as the fashion of the day dictated. He carried a black briefcase at his side, and from the way his shoulder hung low, Karl knew it was heavy.

Karl stiffened slightly. Old habits were the last ones to go. He'd been trained at an early age to put on a regal appearance, to always be better than everyone else in a given room. He was, after all, the heir to one of the most dominant empires in history. Even in defeat, Karl wasn't going to let down a guard that had been forged since the day he was born.

He raised his chin as the two approached and entered the makeshift living room on the right-hand side of the hotel lobby. Here, they would be uninterrupted—not that anyone else would be coming into the hotel for a room.

The place had been evacuated, and the proprietors paid for its use to house the imperial family.

Karl wondered if the taxpayers loyal to the victors knew about that little endowment. Not that he cared. Let them spend their money to feed and house him and his family. They were all beneath him anyway. It was his birthright.

If he'd had his way, and the war won, the world would have been bowing to him.

He released the sense of regret as Johannes stepped onto the rug between the four sofas positioned in a sort of rectangle near the windows. Once more, the servant bowed low and then extended his hand toward the guest.

The man removed his bowler hat—something he probably should have done on the way into the building—and offered a nod of his head. It was a polite gesture, but also one that told Karl the man would not bow to anyone.

That was to be expected from an American. They had a reputation for disregarding royal authority. It was, after all, how their nation had been created.

Karl admired their spirit, to a degree, even though they had been a part of his downfall in the Great War.

The Americans had entered the conflict in the late hours, but their involvement had sealed the fate of those allied with the kaiser. Still, he didn't resent the man standing before him now. Rather, Karl appreciated his willingness to come, particularly because of the salvation he offered.

Money had been in short supply since the imperial family's exile to Madeira from Switzerland. Sure, they had accommodations, food, and a few other niceties, but to someone accustomed to having everything he wanted, it felt like living in squalor. The building would probably be considered a mansion to most, even though it was nothing more than a modest inn with a few nice adornments and furnishings—masks to cover up its ordinary core.

But the money he would receive from this visitor wasn't meant to go to luxuries, spent foolishly on fine wine or food or women. No, Karl had other plans, and this American unwittingly was going to fund them.

"Charles the First of Austria," the American said. His accent hinted at a twang from the American Southeast, though with subtle refinement. "I have to say, it is an honor to meet you, sir. My name is Clarence Gibbs. You know what I do."

Charles was the name many knew him by, his formal title. Karl appreciated the sentiment, and so didn't correct his guest.

"A pleasure," Karl replied. "Yes, I am aware of your position. I do appreciate you coming so quickly."

"An opportunity like this is one not to be missed. My employer insisted I not delay once they received your... invitation. She has a great admiration for history, culture, and art. What you have to offer will make an incredible addition to her family's collection."

"I'm sure it will." His voice sounded dry and snide.

"So, we okay to talk about this here?" Gibbs looked around the room at the guards standing at attention. There were ten in total, four by the exit, four more spaced at wide intervals around the lobby, and two over near a set of doors in the back.

"Yes. These men are not appreciated by their own governments. Their job is an insult to their training, and they know it. They care not what we discuss."

Gibbs shrugged. "If you say so."

He set the briefcase down on the carpet and nudged it toward the former emperor. "It's all in there," Gibbs said. "Count it if you like."

"That won't be necessary, Mr. Gibbs." Karl twirled his right index finger toward Johannes. "Please, bring him the item we promised."

Karl noticed the eagerness in his guest's eyes, the hunger he'd seen before in the pupils of greedy men desperate to get their hands on something they prized.

Johannes bowed, then scurried behind the sofa where his emperor sat. He stooped over an oak chest tucked away underneath a window and between two curtains. He inserted a key into the lock and lifted the lid.

Gibbs watched the servant remove a silver box from the chest and close the lid before returning to his side. He extended the container to the American visitor, who accepted it with both hands.

It was heavy, and his muscles strained immediately to keep from dropping it.

"Thank you," Gibbs said. He looked at Karl, who sat on his sofa with fingers steeped in front of him. "May I...have a look?"

"Of course. You'd be a fool not to."

Gibbs took a deep breath and pried open the lid. The gem within sat on a velvet bed, cushioned on all sides to protect it. The champagne color shimmered in the rays of sunlight that speared through the windows. It was the largest diamond Gibbs had ever seen.

He could hardly believe he was actually holding it—a piece of history that had passed through the hands of some of the most powerful people on the planet for over four centuries.

He closed the lid and nodded. It was authentic. Such a forgery would not pass his expert eyes. Normally, he'd have used a few tools to make certain, but in this case, he knew it was the real deal.

The cuts were perfect, and in keeping with everything he'd read about the diamond.

"My employer will be pleased," Gibbs said. "I am curious, though, if your enemies may come looking for it."

"All the more reason for me to sell it now. They have taken everything from me. Only a matter of time until they took this as well."

"What will you tell them happened to it?"

Karl's lips cracked into a broad, devilish smile. "That I had it cut up and sold in pieces," he answered. "Once it's gone, there's nothing they can do about that. I would rather sell it and keep it preserved by someone who appreciates it. Destroying it would be a pity."

"Sounds like you have a plan."

"The rumor that it was stolen and taken to South America worked well enough. As far as I know, that's what my enemies still believe happened. I doubt they will come around asking for it. Still, it's good to have a plan just in case."

"I know what you mean, sir." Gibbs looked down at the briefcase. "I won't bother asking what you're going to do with five million dollars. That's none of my business." He looked around the lobby again. "But I'm guessing you could keep your family set up in a nice place like this for a long time with that kind of cash."

Karl snorted, though he hid the derision from his guest. He guessed that a place like this would seem like a palace to the American, despite his connections to a prominent buyer.

"Yes. It will do," the former emperor managed. "Thank you for coming. Will you be requiring anything else before you leave? Food? Drink? A bed for the night?"

Gibbs shook his head. "No, thank you, sir. I'm afraid my orders are to get this to my employer as soon as possible. I don't know what they have planned for it."

"It is no longer mine. I care not what they do with it." Karl bowed his head. "Thank you for your business. Johannes will show you out."

Gibbs said his goodbyes, and Karl watched as Johannes escorted him back to the exit and through the doors.

His eyes fell to the briefcase on the floor. He wished he could use the money contained within to fund a revolution of sorts; much the way Napoleon Bonaparte had done over a hundred years prior when he was in exile on the island of Elba.

But that coup had failed, and there was no reason to think that wouldn't happen with Karl, too.

On top of that, he didn't have the numbers of loyal supporters that Bonaparte had. Something scratched in his chest, and the coughing fit returned—harder this time than before.

When he was done, his eyes watered, and resentment filled his heart. This was how he was going to go out—sick, and broke, on a blasted Portuguese island in the Atlantic.

At least the diamond was in good hands, and he had enough money to settle his affairs and take care of the royal family for a long time.

Still, he wondered what would become of the fabled Florentine Diamond. He felt relieved at having sold it, though. It was, after all, only a matter of time until the thieves who'd been trying to steal it from him finally succeeded.

1

ORLANDO, FLORIDA

Darkness enshrouded Sean Wyatt. The tiny, windowless room felt stifling. Dim lights flickered from black chandeliers overhead and on matching aged shelves along every wall.

Sean felt an odd sense of apprehension, nerves tickling his gut with butterfly wings amid roped knots. Normally, indecision was something Sean didn't experience.

His years with the redacted government agency known as Axis had stripped away hesitation in even the direst situations. Something such as this shouldn't have even pinched his mind.

It didn't help that the room was full of innocent people, all being ushered through the corral of rails toward the front.

Eerie eyes stared down at him from creepy portraits hanging along the walls and propped on shelves near books laced with dusty spiderwebs.

The place should have smelled like an old museum, or a library brimming with thousands of dusty old tomes.

Instead, the aromas that taunted the senses of those in the room were that of cookies, cakes, and pastries.

Sean moved ahead through the line.

He'd waited for nearly an hour to get in here, but now that he found himself almost to the counter, the pressure of what to do mounted despite the welcoming, friendly smiles on the faces of those standing behind the registers taking orders.

Gideon's Bakehouse was legendary to those who were lucky enough to be in the know. And those who weren't were usually quickly converted by the sheer number of people walking around with bags of treats from the renowned bakery.

By the time the place opened at ten o'clock in the morning, the line to get in was forty-five minutes deep and wrapped around the block.

Standing inside, staring at the delicacies on offer, Sean mused that the place might serve well as a haunted house. The interior decor certainly skewed that way.

Sean shuffled past the models of cookies and cakes on display and forced himself to check his phone again to make sure he had what he needed. Tommy was, after all, a connoisseur of sweets, and if Sean screwed up the order, he'd hear no end of it from his friend.

He would have told Tommy to get the cookies and cakes himself, but Tommy was preoccupied getting ready for a presentation in the city.

"The things I do for that guy," Sean muttered.

He approached the cashier—a cute young blonde with too much bright red lipstick, a nose ring, and caked on dark eyeshadow. If she was going for goth, the blonde hair shattered those aspirations, but otherwise she fit the bill.

"Hey," she said cheerfully. "What can I get for you today?"

She mirrored the attitude of seemingly everyone who worked here. Despite the ominous, Addams Family-type appearance of the bakery's interior, everyone appeared happy and ready to help the next customer.

Sean figured it was because they were in their true element.

"Hi," Sean said. He set his phone on the counter and turned it around so the girl could read the list. "I need to get these," he said. "Figured it would be easier if I just showed you the list."

"Sure thing. That works." She scanned it quickly and then ducked behind the counter, pulled out a couple of cardboard boxes, and then began filling small paper bags with impossibly thick cookies.

"Excuse me," Sean said. "But how many of these am I allowed to get?"

"Nine," she replied. "Nine per customer."

"Oh. I'm afraid I have too many on there."

She shrugged, winked at him, and leaned forward. "It'll be our little secret," she whispered.

Sean nodded in appreciation, noting the name tag just below her left shoulder. "Thank you, Wendy."

"No problem."

She finished packing the cookies and a slice of cake that looked to be the size of Sean's head, then stuffed the boxes into a huge brown-and-black paper bag.

"Anything else?" Wendy asked.

"No. Thank you. I think that's enough to last a while."

"You have good taste."

He shook his head as he removed a credit card from his money clip. "They're not for me. Well, one is. The rest are for a friend."

She arched an eyebrow at the admission. "Well, do yourself a favor, and at least try a little of each of them. You won't regret it." She rang up the total and gave him the amount due.

He passed the card to her.

"You sure you don't want anything else?" she pressed.

"No, thanks. I'm good. You've been very helpful."

"My pleasure." She took the receipt from the register and placed it on the counter, then picked up a pen and wrote her phone number on the bottom before sliding the paper across to him. "If you change your mind and want something else, give me a call."

Sean's head spun for a second, and he didn't fully grasp what was happening. His voice caught, and he had to clear his throat. "Sorry," he said, holding up his left hand to show off the black tungsten wedding band on his ring finger. "Married, but thank you."

"Oh," she said, only blushing for a second. "Lucky girl. Enjoy those cookies." Her smile never faded as he turned and walked toward the door.

Sean chuckled to himself. The girl was probably half his age. "Still got it, Sean. Still got it."

He pressed the heavy black door open and was immediately blinded by the bright Central Florida sun, along with the late morning humidity that seemed to never go away.

The two young women at the front door smiled and bade him a good day. Sean thanked them, offered the same, and descended the steps. He turned right at the head of the line that still wrapped around the entire block, disappearing past the corner.

People stared at his bag longingly as he walked by, and a few jealous eyes met his with what he thought looked a little like disdain.

"These people really are rabid for this stuff," he mused, glancing down at the heavy bag.

He felt the intense need to get to the parking garage where he'd left his car. The delights in the sack might melt in the swelling heat, even if it was October.

Sean cut to the left and walked past a clothing shop, then over an arched, wooden bridge that spanned a fake pond and stream with a painted concrete base.

The outdoor shopping area played home to high-end clothiers, bars, restaurants, and a variety of other shops for people vacationing to America's most expensive getaway destination.

Sean hadn't come here much as a child. He recalled one visit with his parents, and then again with a girl he dated in college. This outdoor mall wasn't here during his childhood, and was a new attraction in the late 1990s when he'd returned.

At this hour of the day, the wide promenades were still mostly empty, though that would change as the lunch hour drew near.

He found himself wanting a cup of coffee and kept walking straight after crossing the bridge, continuing on the sidewalk past a booth selling sunglasses, another with myriad varieties of socks, and more shops all around.

He caught the aroma of brewed coffee on the dancing wind that funneled and swirled through the open-air corridor before he could even see the shop around the corner.

Sean hoped the line wouldn't be too long yet, but at this time of day he figured that would be the second-longest line in the place behind the bakery he'd just left moments before.

The shop appeared with its signature sign protruding in big, bold white letters across the façade that hung over the counter. Chains dangled from posts in the floor to lead customers through the line before splitting at the front and separating patrons toward one of two registers where orders were taken.

A long line of people waited to the far right at the drink pickup station. That wasn't a good sign—except from the look of the motley crew standing there, Sean guessed that most of them had ordered half-calf, almond milk, no whip, triple-chocolate mocha blended ice coffee.

He rolled his eyes as he approached the surprisingly short line in front of the ordering windows. His drink would only take a minute to make.

Sean started the day with a couple of cups of black coffee, and only ordered a fancy espresso beverage at places he knew could make a good cortado. Despite the fame and household name-level of this joint, Sean had given up on the franchise making those a long time ago.

A man in a red polo and white ball cap placed an order for some kind of chai latte beverage with around sixty modifications, and then stepped around to the corner where the rest of the picky drinkers waited for their orders.

"What drink would pick up your morning?" the young girl asked. Her name tag read Emma and had a couple of smiley face stickers attached to the edges. Her brown hair was pulled back in a ponytail. Her matching eyes were kind, welcoming, and portrayed a joy of working that too few possessed these days.

"Double espresso, please," Sean said with a grin, and whipped out his money clip. He slid the golden card out and passed it to the barista.

"I like your style with the double," she said. He could tell she meant it. "Oh, and this card. I don't see these reward cards much anymore. Everyone just uses the app to pay. But I love these."

"I guess I'm old school," Sean quipped.

"Me too."

He knew she meant that in a retro kind of way, the way kids who'd been born long after a thing was popular started liking that thing because it was old, not necessarily because they loved it. Then again, she didn't seem insincere.

There were a few, like the guy who cut his hair, who truly appreciated the old ways. The guy even had a jet ski from the 1980s because he thought they were better than the ones you sit on.

She ran the card, handed him the receipt, and told him his drink would be up in a moment.

"Thanks, Emma," he said with a polite smile that caused her cheeks to burn red. "Have a lovely day."

"You too," she said with a nervous twinge to her voice.

It was less than two minutes before one of the baristas called out, "Wyatt!"

Sean stepped up to the counter and picked up the little paper cup, once more drawing the ire of the people waiting on their drinks who'd probably ordered ten minutes before him.

He grinned like the devil in a sauna as he turned away from the pickup window. He would have taken a step back out onto the promenade, but a slender woman with black hair blocked his way.

She was gorgeous, with full lips the color of plums, dark eyes that demanded utter attention, and an athletic figure wrapped in a form-fitting black dress and matching high heels.

She looked like a supermodel, at least some he'd seen in pictures, though he'd never actually met one in real life.

"Sean Wyatt?" she said.

Hearing his name caught him off guard. He quickly surveyed his surroundings—old instincts instantly kicking in. He doubted anyone in here was armed. There were metal detectors at all the entrances to the shopping area, though he'd wondered on the way in if there were a few places that someone could slip in with a firearm.

He didn't notice anything or anyone suspicious and met the woman's eyes. "Who's asking?"

He raised the espresso cup to his lips and took a drink, partly to take a second to figure out who this woman was. Nothing came to mind.

"My name is Giulia Agosti," she said. Her accent was unmistakably Italian, and the name reinforced that.

"What part of Italy are you from, Ms. Agosti?"

Her right eyebrow reached up for a second, and her jaw tightened. "Tuscany," she said.

"Nice area."

"Yes. It's beautiful, great food, history, wine, all the things Americans love to talk about."

It sounded like she'd grown tired of the clichéd travel conversation long ago.

"I just meant the scenery," he corrected. "But yeah, all that is good, too." He cocked his head at an angle. "So, it isn't every day that a stranger comes up to me and says my name, particularly in a place I don't frequent. To what do I owe the pleasure?"

Her expression softened, as if she realized she'd been a little harsh before.

"I need your help, Mister Wyatt."

"My help?" He looked around, eyes panning the passing pedestrians amid the sounds of popular dance music pounding from hidden speakers. "What kind of help?"

She reached into a red vinyl purse hanging from her shoulder and pulled out a small photograph. She passed it to him and waited.

Sean took the picture and stared at it for a second. "What is this?" he asked.

"You don't know?"

He shook his head. "Not at first glance, no. But my specialty isn't gemology. I do know a few, though, who might be able to help."

He started to hand the picture back to her, but she didn't extend a hand to accept. "That, Mister Wyatt—"

"Sean. Okay? You're an adult. I'm an adult. Doesn't matter if you're younger than me." He didn't offer a guess as to how much younger, but he figured at least fifteen to twenty years. She looked no older than twenty-eight, tops.

"Very well, Sean. That is a picture of the famous Florentine Diamond."

Sean pulled his hand back with the picture and studied it again. He took another sip of his espresso and hardened his expression. He should have recognized the diamond immediately, but the espresso had yet to kick in. The mind fog evaporated, parting like the sea before a battleship.

"Ms. Agosti—"

"Giulia."

"Fair enough, Giulia. The Florentine Diamond disappeared a long time ago. More than a hundred years ago, actually. I suspect you know that, though, which begs the question: How were you able to get a modern photograph of it?"

"That," she said, pointing at the image, "is a replica. It's on display this week, here in Orlando, where your friend Tommy Schultz is giving a presentation on the history of Florence."

Sean had walked through the exhibit, but he'd only had a few minutes to hang out. He planned on going back this evening and spending more time to fully appreciate the collection on display.

"Seems like you don't need my help after all," he said, passing the photo back to her. "Looks like you found it. Or is the help you need more in the way of getting you into the exhibit this evening? I suppose I could pull a few strings if you—"

"I don't need help getting into the exhibit." Her tone reflected the burning annoyance in her eyes. "I need help finding the original."

2

Sean sat down in a chair facing the front door of the restaurant. It was cool, which made him feel better about the delicacies still packed in the bag he set at his feet.

That didn't mean he wanted to dally around here for hours on end with the Italian woman he'd met only minutes before.

Giulia sat across from him and leaned back in the red wooden chair.

A young man with thick brown hair brushed over to one side approached wearing a white shirt and black trousers.

"Hello," he said kindly. "What can I get for you two?"

"Just coffee," Giulia replied. "No cream."

"And you?" the server asked Sean.

"Same."

The waiter spied the little espresso cup Sean had set on the table in front of him, then shrugged and walked back to the bar.

Sean leaned forward, nudging the cup out of the way. "Okay. You got me here. Now talk."

He wasn't trying to be rude, but he and Tommy were approached semi frequently by amateur treasure hunters bent on tracking down some lost fortune that would set them up financially for life.

Sean didn't assume she was one of those, but she also hadn't proved that she wasn't.

"To the point. I've heard that about you," she confessed.

"From who?"

"We know some of the same people, Sean. I am a historian. Look me up if you want to. Currently, I work for a foundation based in Italy."

"And this... foundation sent you here?"

"Yes. They approved the trip here."

He raised his chin, assessing her body language, tone, looking for any nervous ticks. "How did you know I was going to be in Orlando?"

She crossed one leg over the other knee and leaned her body to the side in a casual display. "I knew Tommy was going to be speaking at the exhibit. That much was easy to find out."

"And finding me here? In this place?"

"I followed you from the exhibit. You dropped off your friend earlier, and I tailed you here. I have to admit: I'm surprised at your sweet tooth."

She passed him a snarky smile.

"They aren't for me. Tommy asked me to come to this place." Sean glanced out the window toward the promenade. The pedestrian traffic had seemingly doubled in the last five minutes.

"It doesn't matter," she said.

The server returned with two cups of coffee and placed one in front of each of them.

"Can I get you anything else? Food menu?"

Sean didn't want to occupy the guy's table and only get a couple of cups of coffee while he could make more money from other patrons, but he wasn't hungry and didn't figure this was going to be a sort of brunch business meeting.

"I think we're fine, thank you," he said.

The waiter seemed unaffected. "No worries. I'll be back to check on you in a few minutes if you change your mind."

Sean waited a second and then returned his attention to Giulia.

"So, what's all this about? You want help trying to track down the real Florentine Diamond?"

She didn't miss the cynicism in his voice. "There is a message on the base of the diamond, the silver part that holds the gem in place."

Sean picked up the red coffee cup and twisted it around so he could grip the handle. He didn't need the extra caffeine, particularly after a double espresso, but if it was in front of him, he might as well have a few sips.

He raised the cup to his lips, took a drink, and set the steaming cup back on its saucer.

"I'm sure that piece has been thoroughly inspected. In fact, I'd wager Tommy analyzed it himself. No one made any mention of a secret message on the bottom of it."

"That doesn't surprise me. The message is innocuous in nature."

"You've seen it?"

"Not with my own eyes. No. And before you ask, I don't know what it says. But I know it's there."

"How?"

Her throat pulsed once as she swallowed. He'd unnerved her, something Sean could tell wasn't easy. "Because the last will and testament of Clarence Gibbs only provided two things. One, that his fortune be given to children's charities."

"And the second?"

She leveled her gaze at him. "Only one sentence. It said, 'The dance of the stone begins at the bottom.'"

Sean waited before saying anything as he considered the line.

"I believe the bottom Gibbs referred to is the base of the replica diamond."

"The dance of the stone," Sean muttered. "Funny thing to say. What kind of dance?"

Flames burned in her eyes, and her neutral expression soured. She stood, as if to leave.

"Sorry," he offered. "I don't mean to sound on edge. It's just that—"

"You get many people coming to you with things like this," she finished. "I understand. I'm not crazy, Sean. I know it's there."

"And you need me to get you a close-up look at it?"

"No." She shook her head. "I want you and Tommy to see it for yourselves. You said your friend probably looked at it. I want him to look again."

Giulia lifted the cup to her lips and took a long sip of the hot coffee.

She watched him over the rim of the mug, waiting to see his reaction. If he was surprised, he didn't show it.

Sean considered her words carefully. There was no inherent danger in doing what she asked. He was heading back to the exhibition anyway. What harm would it do to have a quick peek at the replica and see if it had a mystery to offer?

Curiosity tugged at his mind.

There was still a big question looming, and he wasn't sure how to delicately ask it.

"How do I know you are who you say you are?" Sean asked, deciding to just come out with it. "And suppose you're right. What's in it for you if we were to find the lost diamond?"

She didn't flinch at what could have been an offensive question. Giulia answered as if she'd expected it. "I am like you, Sean. I don't do this for fame or fortune. The Florentine Diamond is an important part of history. To recover it and return it to Tuscany would be to restore a piece of the past that has been forgotten."

That was the answer he'd hoped she'd give, even if it did sound a little rehearsed.

Giulia didn't give him a chance to protest. "The Florentine Diamond disappeared after the death of Charles the First of Austria."

"The last of the Hapsburg Dynasty," Sean added.

"Correct. He died on the island of Madeira, one of the Portuguese islands in the Atlantic."

"Nice place. Not a big fan of their beaches, though. Not enough white sand for me. I'm partial to the Emerald Coast along 30A."

He waited for her to respond, but all he received was a blank stare. His head shook slightly. "Never heard of the Emerald Coast? The Florida Panhandle?" Still nothing.

"Are you talking about beaches right now?" she asked, confused.

"Yeah, you know what, you have beaches in Italy. Keep going. You were talking about the island of Madeira."

Still somewhat derailed, she forged ahead. "Yes. Charles the First died of pneumonia on Madeira, in the city of Funchal. There are rumors about what happened to the stone after his death, but they are inconsistent at best. Some say the diamond went to Argentina, sold to someone there by the former emperor. Others suggest that the diamond ended up with an American buyer and was cut up into pieces and sold off."

"That would make tracking it down slightly more difficult," he joked.

She sighed and kept going. "None of those stories are true. The diamond was sold to an American buyer, but I don't believe it was destroyed."

Sean puzzled over the statement, and he let his face show it.

"How do you know that?" he asked.

She shifted in her seat and took another drink. To Sean, it looked like a body language slipup of discomfort, which usually preceded a lie—at least in his experience.

"I found something during my investigation into the disappearance of the diamond. It was a note from Charles himself. It was in an obscure book on the history of his dynasty, in a chapter about the crown jewels."

Sean leaned forward and rested his elbows on the table. "A note? What did it say?"

She drew a breath and exhaled. "It had the name of a man. Nothing else."

"A name?" He didn't want to insult her, but that was far from a clue.

"Clarence Gibbs."

"Doesn't ring a bell." Sean folded his hands, still keeping his elbows on the table.

She switched legs, crossing them again the opposite way. "It took a lot of research before I could find out anything about the man. His life was, by the scant accounts I could find, unremarkable."

"Seems strange for an ordinary commoner to be named in a book owned by a former emperor. Maybe there was another one?"

"No. I filtered through ship manifests of the time. His name came up."

"How did you—"

"I have my methods, as I know you and your friend do," she cut him off.

Sean sensed she wasn't going to give up this mystery. She'd either hired people to do the grunt work of sifting through century-old passenger manifests, or she'd found a way to hunt for them digitally—perhaps with an AI bot of some kind. Either way, he decided to go with it.

"There must have been something unusual about this Gibbs fellow," Sean insisted.

"Yes. There was. He traveled a lot."

"That's not all that weird. I travel a lot. Seems like you do, too."

"Yes, but I know who you work for. This man didn't have an employer. Not on the record, anyway. And there was nothing about his career in his obituary. What's even odder is the amount of money he left behind."

"He was rich? Who'd he leave it to? Kids?"

"Gibbs never married. So, he had no children to leave the fortune to."

"Nieces or nephews maybe?" Sean guessed.

"He was an only child. No close relations. I suspect whoever he worked for chose him partially for that reason. No attachments."

That was an interesting theory. Sean realized again he was getting reeled in further.

"So, this Gibbs character leaves a clue in his will to something on the base of the Florentine Diamond's replica that will somehow lead to the real diamond, the one that's been missing for a century."

"I can see this was a waste of my time and yours. Good day, Mister Wyatt."

He raised his hand before she could spin around and leave. "Now, I didn't say I wouldn't help. I'm just trying to piece this together. Sit back down. Please. Let's think this through."

Sean wondered how she'd managed to track down the Gibbs' will, but decided details like that could wait. If she'd wanted to get him on the hook, she'd done it.

The waiter came by at an inopportune moment, and asked if they wanted anything else.

"No, thank you," she said, taking a twenty out of her purse and passing it to him. "Keep the change."

Sean looked impressed. "That's a big tip for someone from Europe. Most of my European friends are shocked at how much we leave in tips over here."

"Your workers aren't paid the same in places like these. I know the deal, Sean. When in Rome, no?"

He caught the cute play on words referring to her native country.

"You don't have to do that. I'm happy to—"

"I'm not going to ask for your help and then make you pay for my coffee. I'm not a parasite."

"Well, grazie," he said, raising his mug.

"Prego. I'm afraid I need an answer, Sean. If you won't help me, then I will have to find another way."

Sean delayed his answer for a few seconds, but he'd already made up his mind. He didn't like the sound of her suggesting she would do something under the table to get what she wanted, but there would be no need for that.

He was heading to the exhibition anyway, and it wasn't going to open for another seven hours. That should be more than enough time for him and Tommy to take a look at the diamond and see if there was anything unusual.

"Did you get here in a rental, or did you take an Uber?" Sean asked.

"Uber. Why?" She raised her nose slightly, peering across at him with suspicion.

"Just want to know if you needed a lift, or if you're going to get back to the exhibit on your own."

3

"You're sure about this?" Tommy asked, glancing back over at the woman in the black dress, suspicion dripping from his narrowed eyes.

"Nice outfit, by the way," Sean said, ignoring the question as he gave his friend's outfit a once-over. The navy-blue blazer, light blue button-up shirt, and white pants were definitely off-brand for the usually casual Tommy Schultz. "You look like you're about ready to go on a three-hour tour with Mrs. Howell."

"Hilarious. And thank you. Now I won't be able to get the theme song to *Gilligan's Island* out of my head."

"What are friends for?" Sean chuckled with a shrug.

They stood in the lobby of the exhibit hall, just outside a set of eight black metal doors. Nothing was going on at the moment other than a few last-minute preparations. A couple of workers rolled a cart full of plastic chairs up to one of the doors. One guy pulled open the right door and waited while the other shoved the cart through before following to the other side.

"And yes, I'm sure," Sean said. "What does it hurt? We still have like six hours until the thing starts. The replica is on display, right?"

"Of course. It's one of the centerpieces. But I would have to get the curator to take it out of the glass."

"So, where is the curator?"

"Mr. Schultz," a deep, masculine voice interrupted. "I am sorry to disturb you, but will you be needing anything else?"

Tommy had a goofy look on his face that told Sean this guy was the curator for the event. He was taller than Sean by two inches, towering over both him and Tommy. His nose had a slight arch to it, perched on a slender, sallow face just above a bristly black mustache. His black hair was slicked back with product, and he was already dressed in a tuxedo as if the event started in five minutes.

"Actually," Tommy said. "There is one thing I would like to look at if you don't mind."

The curator raised a curious eyebrow.

Tommy simply smiled politely up at him.

One minute later, they were in the exhibition hall. It was essentially a grand ballroom, complete with crystal chandeliers hanging from the ceiling in two rows. A pair of cash bars were set up on either side of the central aisle leading to a stage at the other end of the room. Between the doors and round tables set for the evening meal stood dozens of glass cases atop white pedestals.

On display within the clear, thick glass were jewels, paintings, pieces of clothing, and other artistic items from the city of Florence dating back to the time of the Medici family.

Tommy and Sean locked in on the one in question, a tall cube-shaped display atop a similarly shaped white plinth.

"This is highly irregular, Mr. Schultz." The curator didn't seem happy about the unusual request.

Tommy had done his best to make it sound like opening up the case and having a look inside was no big deal, but he knew that wasn't true. They'd have to shut off the alarm system, or at least the sensors on the replica diamond's casing, fetch handling gloves, and make sure there was no one around that could come in and snag the item.

"I know," Tommy said. "And I appreciate your help. There's just one more thing I need to confirm."

"Our people have been thorough."

"Yes, I know. This for my curiosity."

While the answer didn't please the curator, it seemed to satisfy him.

He led the three to the pedestal in the center of the room and stopped next to it, where he slipped on a pair of white cotton gloves. "Disarm piece 001," he said into a lapel mic attached to the inside of his white collar.

The curator waited a couple of seconds for confirmation from the person in charge of the alarm system, and then carefully placed his fingers on the glass. He lifted the case gently off the base and lowered it to the floor, leaving the replica diamond exposed.

The man stood near the pedestal and stared at Tommy. "So, what is it you need to see?"

Tommy took a step closer. He leaned in and inspected the sides of the carved silver ornament. The setting was designed to look like a series of silver vines and leaves, with a pair of leaves wrapping around the diamond like a cradle, secured by two tendrils of vine.

"I don't know," Tommy admitted as he stepped around to the other side of the base. He cocked his head sideways to get another angle.

Sean and Giulia watched; eyes glued to the piece.

Tommy straightened and looked to the curator, who now stood with his gloved hands folded in front of his waist.

"Would you mind lifting it up so I can see underneath?" Tommy asked.

The curator sighed, clearly irritated at the additional request.

"Certainly," he allowed, albeit with significant effort.

He stepped closer and cautiously placed his fingers around the bottom of the silver sculpture and lifted.

The man tilted it enough for Tommy to see the underside.

"There's an address," Tommy stated. "It's in Buenos Aires."

"Argentina?" Sean clarified.

"Yeah. And there's a date, too: 1921. Along with the words *Inizia la danza degli inganni*." He held up his phone and took a picture of the setting's bottom. "That's an odd sort of thing to include here. What does that mean?"

"Deception's dance begins," Giulia replied.

The curator's arms strained from holding the heavy object, and his face tensed with a little vein popping up on his right temple.

"Have you seen enough?" he asked.

"Oh, sorry," Tommy offered. "Yeah. Set it down."

The man eased the casing back onto the pedestal. He quickly inspected the sides to make sure the shiny metal hadn't been smudged, then lifted the glass case back into place.

"Will you be needing anything else, Mister Schultz?" the curator asked.

"No, that's all. Thank you."

He bobbed his head once as if to say a reluctant "you're welcome" and then spoke into his mic. "Arm 001," he ordered, and then walked away from the display, leaving the other three alone.

When he was out of earshot, Sean turned to his friend. "That guy's a ray of sunshine."

Tommy chuckled, watching after the curator as he disappeared through the big doors and back into the lobby. "Normally he's not so bad. I think I saw him smile earlier this morning. But he was holding a cronut, so maybe that was why. Speaking of...." Tommy's eyes fell to the bags clutched in Sean's fists. "I say we dive into some of those cookies with some coffee. Hope the line wasn't too much trouble."

"That place is a madhouse. But it was fine. I just hope these cookies are worth the effort."

"Oh, they are. Guaranteed."

"Excuse me," Giulia interrupted. "Are you two going to talk about the inscription on the base of that?" She pointed to the replica.

"Yes. Sorry," Sean offered.

"It's definitely interesting," Tommy added. "But what could it mean? Deception's dance?"

She looked bewildered and dropped her hands out to her sides.

"Don't you two find it the least bit curious that this thing was made in Florence, Italy, but has an address from Argentina inscribed on the bottom? And as far as deception's dance, that must be a reference to the diamond's decoy. That decoy." She emphasized her theory by pointing a finger at the display case.

The two men glanced at each other, both reeled into the mystery. She made a good point, and her hypothesis checked enough boxes to pique their interest, and take them from dubious to curious.

"It's not nothing," Tommy said. "Unless the crafter of the setting simply wanted to name his artwork."

"Deception's dance is a strange name for something that has nothing to do with dancing," Sean countered.

"Fair enough. But what do you propose we do about it? Take off to Argentina because of an address and an unusual note carved into the bottom of a diamond setting?"

"Crossed my mind. But then you wanted to talk about cookies."

"What? First, don't try to throw me under the—"

"Boys, please," she snapped. "Do either of you know anything about the address on the base?"

They quickly sobered their tone.

"No," both said at the same time.

"The date is significant, though," Tommy said. "That was the last time the real Florentine Diamond was seen. Interesting this replica was created then as well."

"Yes," she agreed. "Interesting is a mild way of putting it. Surely, you must see that this is no coincidence."

"She's right, Schultzie," Sean agreed. "It's suspicious. You can't tell me this doesn't make you wonder."

"I've heard the stories," Tommy said. "The tales of how the original made its way to Argentina, and then was cut up and sold off. And I've also heard the rumors about it coming to the United States. I haven't found any credible evidence for either."

Giulia wasn't backing down. "I suggest we find out what we can about that address. It must mean something. The maker in Florence would not have put it on there for no reason."

She took out her phone and started tapping on the screen.

"What are you doing?" Tommy asked.

"Doing a search for the address. Could you please give it to me?"

"Sure." He shook his head, realizing the woman wasn't going to take no for an answer. He looked at his phone and read off the numbers, the street name, and the other details included with the inscription.

She finished typing in the address and then hit the Search button.

Sean moved over to her side and looked down at her phone. The results populated within seconds.

"It's just a house?" she muttered.

Tommy hummed thoughtfully at the revelation. "A house. Deception's dance, 1921. Buenos Aires. I'm going to be honest. I got nothin'."

"Maybe," Sean hedged. He took his phone out of a front pants pocket and tapped on the app that connected him directly to the IAA's artificial intelligence, also known as Malcom. "Malcom, I need you to find any information you can about this address." He gave the street name and number, as well as the city, before adding, "Prioritize ownership history and what was in that location in the year 1921."

"What are you doing?" Giulia asked. "Who's Malcom?"

"AI," Tommy answered for his friend. "We created it a few years ago. Now it seems everyone is using AI for something. But we like to think ours is ahead of the game. Most of the ones available to the public have limited databases, sometimes with out-of-date information. Malcom can track down far more than those publicly available tools. I won't get into the details of how. Frankly, I don't understand half of it. I leave that to our team in the lab."

She looked dubious but accepted the answer nonetheless. "So, you think this Malcom is going to be able to figure out who lived in this place back then?"

"Maybe."

He stared at the device.

Three blinking dots appeared in the text bar for a second before Malcom responded, both speaking in a remarkably human voice and with text on the screen. "This address currently belongs to Isabella

Fernandez. The home has belonged to her family since 1908, and was passed down to her by her father, Armelio Fernandez. He inherited it from his father, Osorio Fernandez."

Sean read the response to the others.

Tommy turned to Giulia. "You ever heard that name before?"

"No. I haven't." Giulia wore a pensive look but added nothing else.

No one said anything for a minute until Sean finally broke the silence. "It might be worth looking into, Schultzie. I don't have anything pressing going on right now other than being here."

Tommy questioned his friend with a sidelong glance. It was an expression of disbelief. "So, you're actually thinking of going down to Argentina? Based on the inscription on the bottom of that?" He jerked his thumb toward the replica.

Sean shrugged. "We've done more for less," he defended. "And this is kind of our thing."

Both Sean and Giulia could see Tommy was toying with the idea in his mind.

"True. And it is definitely curious." He faced Giulia. "Do you really think this is the start of a trail of bread crumbs that will lead to the real Florentine Diamond?"

"I can't say for certain. But if we have a lead, no matter how thin it might be, should we not at least take a closer look? I flew here from Italy just to have a look at this." She indicated the display case containing the fake diamond. "Argentina is just another flight. So, I'm going whether you two join me or not."

Tommy looked back at the replica, then to her again. "You'd probably make a good IAA agent. If you didn't already have a job."

She permitted a smile at the compliment.

"We can take the jet," Tommy said to Sean. "I'll call and make sure it's ready to go." He shook his head. "What a strange life we live, you and I."

"Wake up in Orlando and then fly to Buenos Aires on a lark the same day?"

"Yeah," Tommy said with a chuckle. "Not a lot of people live that way. I'll have to tend to things here for the day, and then I have the presentation tonight, but we can leave after that. I'm not staying for the festivities tomorrow."

"Looks like we're at it again."

"So it would seem." Tommy directed his next words to Giulia. "Get your things."

Giulia beamed, surprised at their sudden decision to help her. "Thank you," she said. "So, you're serious about flying to Argentina after your presentation tonight?"

"Unless you know a better way to visit that house and talk to the homeowner."

"Talk to the homeowner?"

Sean grinned at her. "He's right. There must be something about the address. Maybe this Isabella person knows something. Or we just stay here and forget all about it. Up to you."

The two men watched as the gears turned in Giulia's eyes. "Is this how you two always operate? You just decide in a matter of seconds to fly around the world investigating leads?"

"You sound reluctant. But yeah. Pretty much."

"Okay," she said after another few seconds of thinking. "I'll go get my things at the hotel."

"If it's all right, I'll give you a lift."

"Are you sure? You're already doing so much."

Sean nodded. "Compared to flying to the Southern Hemisphere, this is nothing." He winked then looked at his friend. "We'll meet you back here later," Sean said to Tommy.

"Excellent," Tommy said as he took out his phone and began texting the pilot.

Sean took a deep breath and sighed. "Been a while since I've been to Argentina. Hopefully, this time is less dramatic than the last."

Tommy finished his text and looked down at the bags dangling from Sean's hands. "Yeah, just make sure you leave those cookies with me."

4

Barone Totti watched the hotel building from the driver's seat of his black four-door sedan. He'd parked behind a hedgerow to conceal his position.

The woman he'd been following had gone into the exhibition hall with the man she'd met—apparently—at the outdoor shopping area.

Totti had been assigned to tail Giulia Agosti, and he had done an impeccable job of it up to this point.

His organization, the Rossi Clan, had kept a close eye on her in Italy from the moment she began snooping around, hunting for clues to the whereabouts of the real Florentine Diamond.

The head of the family, Lorenzo Rossi, had been correct in his assessment of the woman. She was clever and resourceful and would stop at nothing to recover the fabled diamond, wherever its current location. A diamond that Lorenzo desperately wanted for his own.

He claimed that his family had ties to the powerful House of Medici that had been so prominent during the Renaissance in Italy. It was a claim that Totti had never looked into, nor did he care to. His boss paid him well, and Totti's loyalty had helped him climb the ranks in the organization.

Some of Rossi's other enforcers had experience in the military, or law enforcement, and had turned to the family for better pay and better upward mobility—albeit with a few cons that always loomed. Not knowing who you could trust was a big one.

Totti, however, didn't have such experience. He'd grown up on the streets, barely raised by his grandfather from the age of eight when his parents were caught in the crossfire of a mob hit in Palermo.

Totti kept a keen eye on Agosti and the American as they pulled out of their parking spot and drove away from the exhibition center. He calmly pressed the ignition button, and the engine revved to life. Then he backed out of his parking spot and turned onto the street, keeping a safe distance behind his mark.

He'd taken pictures of the American as he and Agosti left the outdoor shopping mall. It had surprised Totti to see the woman leave with the man, but he quickly surmised that the American had been the reason she'd gone to the shopping district in the first place.

Totti didn't know who the man was—not at first—but he'd sent a picture of him to his contacts within the organization, and before he'd arrived at the exhibition center received a text message with a concise dossier on the man.

His name was Sean Wyatt, a security and recovery specialist with the International Archaeological Agency based in Atlanta, Georgia. Apparently, this Wyatt character was considered dangerous. A note had been attached to the dossier suggesting that Totti use extreme caution if dealing with Wyatt.

Totti always operated that way. It's what had kept him alive during his upbringing on the streets. He'd seen others fall by the wayside, often as the result of nothing more than sheer carelessness. One such victim had been a friend—in as much as someone like him could have a friend. Totti recalled seeing Giancamo's eyes staring lifelessly up at the sky, blood soaking his gray button-up shirt riddled with bullet holes.

Giancamo had underestimated a debtor to the Rossi Family, and had ended up dead as a result.

Totti made sure the killer took a long time to die as payback for the death of his friend, a death that proved to be a cautionary tale for anyone who ever worked for the family.

Totti allowed a few cars to merge into the lane ahead of him to give an extra buffer to the vehicle he was tailing. He could still see them up ahead and easily followed as they merged onto the ramp to get on the I-4.

He maintained a safe distance for the next five minutes until the car indicated it was exiting the highway.

"Looks like they're going back to her hotel," he muttered to himself. A hint of judgement frayed his tone. He continued following the car until it turned into a hotel parking lot. The driver steered the vehicle into a spot near the main entrance, while Totti veered around them and drove to a spot closer to the back.

He found an empty slot underneath a pair of palm trees and backed his car in so he could leave at a moment's notice if necessary.

He cracked the windows and killed the engine and resumed watching as Agosti exited the car, leaving Wyatt behind in the driver's seat.

"What are you doing?" he wondered.

5

Sean kept his eyes on Giulia until she disappeared inside the hotel lobby. He'd offered to accompany her up to her room to assist with getting her things, but she'd declined, and he hadn't pressed the issue. The last thing he wanted to be was insistent to the point it started to seem inappropriate.

Still, it was in his nature to be protective, and now that they were going to be flying to Argentina together, he felt a certain sense of responsibility in making sure Giulia was okay.

His wife, Adriana Villa, was out of the country—as was so often the case—this time conducting research into a particularly valuable piece of art that had gone missing during World War II.

They shared a mutual understanding of each other's occupations, but more and more he felt the need to be away from her less. He'd never loved anyone so much as he loved Adriana, and as he grew older, Sean felt as though every minute they spent apart was a minute lost.

Sean crammed the last bite of the Oreo-stuffed cookie into his mouth and chewed slowly. Tommy was right. It was the best cookie he'd tasted in his entire life. And Tommy would never let him hear the end of it once Sean let on.

He could see why the line outside the bakery was so long, why people waited for hours to get a couple of bags loaded with the culinary treasures.

Sean looked down the row toward the back of the parking area. A car had gone in behind them and parked in an empty place under a couple of palm trees probably twenty cars down. The driver, however, had not left his seat behind the wheel. Not that Sean had noticed, at least.

Sean couldn't see the driver through the myriad vehicles between them. Perhaps they had slipped in through a side entrance.

Either way, he registered the note in his mind, just in case.

He waited patiently, returning his thoughts to Adriana and his longtime dream of retiring to the coast along the Florida Panhandle. From here, in Orlando, it was about six hours away to where he wanted to be, which was no closer than from Chattanooga, and an hour farther from his place in Atlanta.

Sean had tried to call it quits once. He'd opened a kayak and paddle board shop in Destin, and done all he could to forget his past —and all the ghostly faces that came with it.

He'd never felt regret over the killings. The people whose lives he'd taken were vicious, and would have harmed innocent people had he not intervened with lethal force. Those faces weren't what bothered Sean. It was the one that stared back at him in the mirror every day that haunted him most.

He was a monster, a tool sharpened for an unholy task.

The world needed people like him, though, whether the world cared to admit it or not. Because the truth was it took a monster to fight a monster, and there were plenty of bad ones out there, always hiding in the shadows, waiting for the opportune moment to reveal themselves.

Sean checked the clock on the dashboard. Giulia had been inside for four minutes. He didn't know why, but it felt longer than that.

He pressed his fingers into the tops of his legs and took a couple of long, deep breaths. He didn't know why he felt so on edge, so impatient. It had just set in as he watched Giulia enter the hotel. Like an abrupt wave of anxiety had crashed into him on a day the seas of emotions had seemed so calm and peaceful.

Maybe he was overprotective—even to a person who was essentially a complete stranger.

That reminded him.

Sean took his phone out and performed a quick search on Ms. Giulia Agosti. He probably should have done that before but had taken the woman at her word for the most part. Vetting someone who claimed to be who she was, and who worked for who she claimed, would be a simple enough task, and a difficult lie to sustain for very long. So, he'd given her a little slack.

He entered her name, along with a few keywords, and waited for the results.

Giulia's face appeared next to a bio from her agency in Italy. He tapped on the link, and proceeded to quickly skim through her information.

He didn't need her life story, just to know that she was who she said she was, and from the details on the Italian agency's site, she'd been truthful with him.

Sean noticed movement at the front door to the hotel and looked up. It was a man in a business suit pulling a rolling bag behind him.

He closed out the search on his phone and placed the device in the cup holder in the center console.

Sean knew he couldn't do this forever. He still had plenty of good years left in him, but he knew the horizon was approaching faster by the minute. Would he be able to settle down? Could he be a retiree that sat around on the beach, sipping margs or playing golf three days a week?

He doubted it. And travel would be redundant, though he figured seeing the world again through a different lens might do him some good.

"What are you thinking," he mused.

He could think about retirement another day, a day far off in the distance from right now.

Still in his mid-forties, he had plenty of juice left in him.

He peered through the windshield, watching the front doors to the hotel. A few guests pulled up to the front and unloaded their luggage. More were arriving than departing. It was nearly the weekend, so that made sense. Orlando was not only home to the most-visited theme parks in the world but played host to meetings, seminars, workshops, and sporting events. And that didn't include the many dignitaries and high-profile visitors that would be attending tonight's exhibit.

A man in a gray sport coat, white button-up shirt, and gray slacks walked into view from Sean's right. The guy was wearing aviator sunglasses to shield his eyes from the blazing sun. He was lean, athletic, and tanned. The five o'clock shadow on his face looked intentional, accentuated by a clean-shaven neck. He looked like he'd jumped straight off the cover of *GQ* and onto the pavement.

Sean noted all the details within two seconds but paid especially close attention to the way the man walked and the suspicious way he turned his head back and forth, as if afraid he was being watched. Sean glanced down at the empty cookie wrapper next to him as the guy passed and looked his way.

Had he noticed him? So what if he had?

Sean looked back up, and was about to dismiss his paranoia when he saw the man's jacket flap up in the breeze, exposing the pistol tucked into a concealed holster inside his belt.

"Great," he muttered.

Sean didn't know how he'd missed the tail, though he hadn't been as vigilant as he could have been. His mind, while usually alert to trouble, had been on other things, and up until now he hadn't had a reason to be concerned.

He reached over to the door handle and gently pulled it, then nudged the door open without making more than a muted clicking sound. He paused, watching the man continue to the front door to the hotel, ignoring the valet who greeted him with a pleasant smile that immediately turned sour at the rude gesture.

Sean slid out of the car, shut the door, and scurried across the lane to the walkway leading from the asphalt to the entrance. A wide awning loomed over the drop-off where people unloaded their vehicles, and the instant Sean reached the shade he felt ten degrees cooler.

"Good morning," the valet said, having recovered from the slight from the previous guest.

"Morning," Sean said with a pleasant nod.

The automatic doors opened, parting in the center. Cool air blasted out from the lobby, casting a chilly blanket over Sean's skin as he walked in.

He swept his gaze across the room, taking in a lounge to his immediate right, a collection of tables and chairs along with an empty buffet counter, then the concierge desk to the left.

A cluster of tourists stood in the center of the walkway leading to the elevators just beyond the bar at the lounge. Sean stepped to his left to see beyond them, and found the man he was looking for.

Mr. GQ was headed for the elevators. Once he was on the lift, Sean had no way of knowing where he was going, and stopping him from reaching Giulia in time would take more than just a little luck. It would be nearly impossible.

Sean hurried around the group, doing his best not to look like he was in a hurry.

The man Sean followed seemed to be walking with a sense of urgency as he neared the elevator atrium. The second the guy disappeared around the corner, Sean picked up his pace. The second he got on one of the lifts, it was over.

He cursed himself for not getting Giulia's room number. That would have been an awkward ask, and coming up with an explanation as to why he needed it would be a creative endeavor in its own right.

He could have asked for her phone number, in case she needed help with something, but that, too, would have come across as odd. The truth was he hadn't even considered either of those things. This should have been a simple stop. She goes in, gets her things, comes back out to the car, and they return to the exhibition center.

Why did everything have to be so bloody difficult?

Sean reached the elevator waiting area and rounded the corner. The man, along with a couple with two small children and a woman in a tennis outfit, stood in the atrium awaiting the next elevator.

An up arrow above the lift to the right glowed white, and then Sean heard a ding indicating the elevator had arrived.

The silvery metallic doors opened, and the people inside stepped off and around into the lobby.

Giulia was the last to leave the lift. She pulled a small burgundy suitcase and carried a gray backpack over one shoulder, along with a black makeup bag in her free hand. She eased past the doors and the people waiting to get aboard, and stopped when she saw Sean standing on the fringe of the group.

The others started getting onto the elevator, including the man he'd been following. The guy had taken off his sunglasses and made his way through the doors in an orderly, calm manner.

"Sean?" Giulia said. Her confused frown told him what she was thinking before she said it. "What are you doing in here?"

Sean waited three heartbeats as the doors closed and the elevator took off toward the second floor.

"I... just thought maybe you needed some help. So, I was going to come... see if you did."

The puzzled expression on her face only grew stronger. "But you don't know what room I was in. How would you have come to help me?"

"Right," Sean said, pointing at her as if she'd answered a game show question. "I didn't think of that until I got here to the elevators." He looked down at her luggage. "I don't suppose you do need any help, do you?" Sean felt like an idiot, and knew he probably looked the part, too.

"No, I'm fine. Thank you."

She left the sentence hanging there, and in the meantime the second lift arrived. The bell dinged and snapped Sean out of his awkward trance. "Great. Okay then. Let's get going."

He rounded toward the exit with his cheeks burning from embarrassment. Halfway through the lobby, he glanced back toward the elevator. He'd been so wrong about the man he followed into the hotel.

It was moments like that Sean felt like he was losing his touch, like the edge he'd leaned on for more than a decade was now blunted from overuse.

The doors parted, and the two walked through. Sean nodded to the valet again. The man bade them a good day with a cheerful wave of the hand.

Sean and Giulia crossed the thoroughfare back to the row of cars and veered left, walking toward their parking spot.

Sean took the key fob out of his pocket and clicked the unlock button twice.

A warm breeze blew through the lot. The palm trees lining the edge just behind the curve waved gently, the huge heaves rustling against one another as they overlapped.

Sean pressed another button on the fob, and the trunk of the car clicked and opened.

"I'll take those," he said, and turned to relieve Giulia of her belongings.

Sean froze.

Giulia's face was pale with fear, her eyes full of panic. The man Sean had seen before was standing just behind her, his right hand hidden in the small of her back.

"Get in the trunk," the man ordered in a thick Italian accent. "Now."

6

Sean knew the man held a gun to her back. The assailant stood at such an angle that no one behind him, or driving into the parking lot from the street, would see. To them, it would appear as if three people were saying their goodbyes before leaving the hotel.

Sean noticed a tattoo on the inside of the man's wrist. It was a circle with an R in the center. It wasn't a small leap to reach the conclusion that this guy was from the Rossi Clan.

"At least my instincts were correct," Sean muttered.

"Get in the trunk. If I have to tell you again, she dies here."

Sean knew the guy was bluffing. He couldn't risk shooting an innocent person in broad daylight in the middle of a populated area. But there was always the 1 percent chance that he was wrong. What if the gunman had nothing to lose, or was reckless and willing to take the risk of shooting her, and then him?

Even if Sean had his Springfield XD on him, he couldn't have drawn it fast enough to save Giulia. The only option at the moment was obedience.

Still, he felt the magnetic pull of his firearm tucked under the driver's seat only a short eight feet away.

"Okay," Sean said, raising his hands out to his sides in a show of surrender. "Take it easy." He moved slowly, cautiously, as he would were he stepping around a venomous snake coiled and ready to strike.

As he backtracked toward the rear of the car, the gunman followed, forcing Giulia forward. Her wide, terror-filled eyes remained fixed on Sean as if pleading for him to do something, anything, that could get her away from this man. But there was nothing he could do.

Even Sean Wyatt had his limitations.

He felt his way backward with his heels, only willing to risk a slight turn of his head to make sure he didn't trip. He stopped when he felt the back of his shoe bump against the curb. The trunk was to the right in front of him.

"Get in," the man ordered again.

Sean resented his position, and he found himself loathing the guy for getting the better of him. The only thing that was saving Sean and Giulia for the moment was being out in the open. Cars drove by on the street to Sean's left. And two valets stood behind a podium while a bellhop stacked luggage onto a cart. None of them knew what was going on.

Another breeze rolled through the lot. This time, it blew the scent of the gunman's cologne straight through Sean's nostrils. He recognized the odor, though it seemed the assailant had seriously overdone the application.

"Bulgari?" Sean asked, twitching his nose. "One spray, man. Two at most. Otherwise, you're overdoing it."

The gunman shoved the gun deeper into Giulia's back. She winced from the jabbing pain.

"Get in." There was no messing around in his voice.

Sean wished he could see the man's eyes, but the aviators blocked that little detail. Not that it mattered. Sean would recognize him if their paths crossed again. He'd already decided he would do whatever it took to make sure that happened.

Sean glanced into the back of the car. *At least I got the sedan with a good-size trunk,* he thought. There was enough room for him to fit, albeit slightly curled up. It would be far from comfortable.

"Any chance you could leave me with a bottle of water?" Sean asked. "It's really hot out here."

He knew he wouldn't last long in the back of the trunk in the oppressive Central Florida heat.

"Now," the gunman demanded. The pained look on Giulia's face worsened to the point that tears pooled in the corners of her eyes.

"Please," she begged through clenched teeth. "Help me."

Sean could only nod, and pray silently for some kind of miracle. Normally, he could make the impossible happen, but this time he felt like his luck had finally run out.

The sound of a car motor and tires rolling on the asphalt filled his ears. The high pitch of brakes that needed to be replaced followed.

Sean twisted his head an inch to the right and watched as a white Toyota minivan eased past them into the empty parking spot beside his car. A man in his midthirties drove, with his wife on the passenger side, and two small children in the back. The rear window had a neatly applied row of one of those stick-figure families, each representing an occupant of the car—including a dog—and each wearing a pair of oversize mouse ears.

No way Sean was getting into the trunk now. The little boy—he guessed to be around seven years old—and his slightly older sister across from him both stared at Sean as if he were in giant mascot costume waiting to welcome them.

The gunman said nothing, but Sean knew the man was probably doing his best to be patient with the change of circumstances. One second, he'd been in complete control, about to rid himself of a problem. The next, he had a family of four naively, innocently driving up and plopping themselves directly in his way.

The driver killed the engine and opened his door. The wife on the other side stepped out as well, and both stretched their arms over their heads before the father pressed a button inside the vehicle that automatically opened both of the rear sliding doors.

Both the kids cheered and kicked their legs.

The father noticed Sean and the other two standing awkwardly behind the trunk of the sedan.

"Oh sorry," the man said as his son hopped out onto the pavement. "I should have waited until you got in."

"No problem," Sean said. "This guy was going to make me get in the trunk anyway."

The father laughed.

Sean had already noted the minivans plates from Indiana. "Long drive for vacation, huh?" he asked.

The father wore a look of utter exhaustion melded with relief. "Yeah. We stopped in Tennessee on the way here and stayed the night before coming the rest of the way. I can't do a trip like that all in one leg."

"I hear you. What part of Tennessee?"

"Chattanooga. Nice town."

"No kidding," Sean chuckled. "That's where I'm from."

"Small world."

The wife walked around the back of the minivan and opened the rear door. The cargo area overflowed with suitcases, overnight bags, discarded sacks from gas stations, and children's toys.

As the husband and father drew near, Sean extended his hand. "Sean Wyatt. Welcome to Orlando. Y'all here to go to the parks?"

While the dad shook his hand, the kids shouted simultaneously. "Yeah!"

"Well, I'm sure you're going to have a great time. And I'm sure your parents' wallets are going to be a lot thinner when you get home."

The dad chuffed. "You got that right. Name's Tom. Tom Sanderson, by the way."

"These are my friends Giulia and her husband Beaumont. But everyone calls him Pookie."

Tom clearly couldn't see where the moniker came from, but he reached out to shake their hands anyway.

Sean smiled as he watched Giulia uneasily clasp the man's hand and shake it timidly. What he really enjoyed was watching their assailant try to conceal his weapon in his pants without raising suspicion before accepting the stranger's obligatory handshake. He clenched his jaw as if he'd just swallowed a spoonful of bitter medicine, then extended his hand.

Tom frowned at the feeble handshake, and when he was done, he leaned in closer to Sean. "Your pal here has a handshake of a dead fish."

"He's an interior designer. Works alone most of the time. So, he doesn't meet many people."

"Ah," Tom said, nodding.

"Looks like you guys have a lot of luggage. Would you like some help getting your stuff to the front?"

"I don't want to be any trouble," Tom said. "I probably should have pulled around to the front drop-off first."

"That's what I said," the wife chimed in.

"Sorry," Tom offered. "This is my wife, Judy. And yes, she's right. She did tell me that."

"We can grab you a cart if you like," Giulia said, joining Sean's offer.

"That would be so kind," Judy replied. "Thank you so much."

"No trouble at all," Sean said. "Pookie, do you want to start the car? We'll be right back."

The gunman stewed but couldn't say anything. All he could do was watch while Giulia and Sean walked back toward the front of the hotel.

Sean didn't like the idea of leaving the guy there with the family from Indiana, but he doubted the Italian assassin would try anything with them.

"What's your plan?" Giulia asked as they approached the hotel entrance.

"We're going to get a cart," Sean answered with a look back over his shoulder. "His little plan is screwed now."

Tom was trying to talk to the gunman, but the guy wasn't having any more of it. He abruptly turned and walked off to the left toward the back of the parking lot, Sean assumed to the car he'd arrived in.

Sean and Giulia walked through the sliding doors again, found a push cart parked next to three others just inside to the left, and then rolled it back out into the parking area.

Sean peered to his left into the parking lot but didn't see where their assailant had gone.

When they were back at the minivan, Tom beamed as he finished unloading the luggage. "Thank you so much for doing that. You really shouldn't have."

"No, I really wanted to. Happy to help."

"Pookie excused himself and went that way. Maybe he needed the toilet."

"Probably," Sean said. "He's had the runs for a few days. Too much shellfish, I think."

"Whoa! TMI, my man," Tom laughed.

"Hey, it was nice to meet you," Sean said. "Have a wonderful vacation. I'm sure you will."

"Nice to meet you, too. Safe travels. And thanks again for the cart."

Sean opened the door for Giulia in the front-passenger side then stepped around to the driver-side door and climbed in. He started the car and waited until the family had loaded the cart and was out of the way, then backed out and drove out of the lot.

The second they hit the street, he took out his phone and called Tommy.

It rang four times before Tommy answered. "Hey, man. What's up?"

"Schultzie, change of plans."

7

BUENOS AIRES

Sean rapped on the door and stepped back to wait. Knocking on a stranger's door had always been a delicate thing to him. He loathed doing it when he was in elementary school during that magical time of year called fundraising.

He and the other kids had carried their cardboard briefcases painted to look like metal around the local neighborhoods to hawk crap that people could get for cheaper somewhere else—but with the promise that the money was going to help their school.

Not that the money didn't go for that.

But Sean hated selling. He hadn't been a salesperson at any moment in his life, especially in his youth. And found the idea of knocking on a stranger's door or ringing their doorbell to be pushy and probably annoying to the homeowner.

He never knew how hard to knock. Too firm, and it sounded demanding, like an angry ex or the cops showing up unexpectedly.

Too soft, and the resident wouldn't hear.

"Do you think she's home?" Giulia asked, interrupting his train of thought.

He didn't know, and was about to step forward and knock again.

The sound of movement inside the home signaled his middle-of-the-road approach had at the very least been heard by the occupant.

"I guess so," he said.

The house was one of the more uniquely painted homes Sean had ever seen. The window frames were bright green, surrounded by shutters of yellow and outer walls painted Carolina blue. It was squeezed between a purple-and-white house to the right and a yellow-and-orange one to the left—all part of the same structure.

Isabella Fernandez's house was one door down from a street corner in old La Boca town, a truly unique barrio near the port of Buenos Aires.

Sean had conducted some research on the long flight down since there was only so much sleep he could get on a plane, and with ten hours to fill, he had to do something other than watch in-flight movies.

The neighborhood saw an influx of Asian and European immigrants in the early twentieth century, the latter primarily coming from Italy—specifically the Liguria region. Sean didn't let that last little detail slip by him. Any connection to Italy and the Florentine Diamond had to raise some flags, and it certainly added to the probability that somehow the original diamond had made its way here.

He'd also tried to learn as much as he could about Isabella's ancestors, but there wasn't much to go on beyond the names. The recordkeeping from those days wasn't in any database Malcom could access, and an internet search engine was even more useless. All that meant if Sean were going to learn anything useful, he'd have to get it directly from Isabella.

A lock clicked from the inside the house, and Sean stiffened.

The door creaked, opening a few inches so the woman inside could peek out. A tarnished brass chain tensed around her eye level.

"Who are you?" she asked in Spanish, her face still mostly concealed in shadow.

"My name is Sean Wyatt, and this is Giulia Agosti," Sean answered back in the woman's native tongue. He knew the names would mean nothing to her. "Are you Isabella Fernandez?"

Her eyelids squeezed tight, eyes analyzing the strangers standing in her doorway. The woman inched toward the opening. The light striped across her face and hair. From the sliver of a view, Sean figured Isabella was in her mid-sixties. The bright red dress draped over her shoulders had a blue, white, and yellow collar—a fabric mosaic of some kind, perhaps a tribute to the original inhabitants of the land.

Isabella wore black glasses with floral patterns on the temples that stretched back to her light blonde hair. Her sky-colored eyes gleamed in the light.

There was a brightness to her, one that mirrored itself in her choice of clothing and apparel.

The locket dangling from her neck was the only accessory that seemed out of place with everything else.

It was old and scuffed, inscribed with two letters on the front: *Y P*. It hung by an unremarkable silver chain. Sean guessed the thing must have been an heirloom.

"I know this is strange. And I apologize for arriving on your doorstep unannounced. But I didn't know how to get in touch with you. I couldn't find your phone number."

She smiled at him as she would a strange dog, begging for food. "How can I help you, Sean Wyatt?"

He took a deep breath, suddenly feeling extremely awkward, and intrusive. "I work for the International Archaeological Agency in the United States, and my colleague here is with an agency based in Italy. We are investigating a significant piece of history that went missing over one hundred years ago."

Isabella frowned with suspicion. "I do not have anything like that," she said, her tone defensive.

The door started to close, the darkness swallowing the vibrant colors of her dress.

"No, wait," he pleaded. "Please. We have a question. It's about your grandfather."

Isabella paused, the door stopping halfway to the frame. "My grandfather?"

Hope widened Giulia's eyes as she saw curiosity pause the woman's retreat.

"Yes," Sean said. "It's about the dance of the stone."

The statement caught her breath as she sucked in air with a quick, subtle gasp.

The door widened again, this time farther than before. "What do you know about that?"

Sean shook his head, trying to convey as much honesty as he could. He had no idea if this woman had been bothered for her entire life over this, or if he were the first one who'd come knocking. "We don't know much, truthfully. We were hoping you could help us out with some of the details."

She studied him for a minute that felt like an hour. She glanced at Giulia, assessing her quickly. Then, finally, she surrendered by unlatching the chain.

Sean wasn't sure he would have let himself in if he'd been on the other side of the door. Crazy American guy claiming to work for some obscure archaeology agency? He liked to think he would at least ask for some form of ID. He figured having Giulia with him probably helped with the trust factor.

"It wasn't my grandfather," Isabella said, the words catching Sean off guard.

"I'm sorry?" Giulia spoke for him, the first thing she'd said to the Argentine woman.

"You are mistaken in regard to my grandfather."

That didn't sound good. They'd traveled all the way down here under the assumption that her grandfather was a key piece to solving the Florentine pursuit. Then again, Sean felt like he should have remembered what happened when one assumed. That adage seemed to never fail.

He saw the rest of her dress, covered in white, yellow, and pink flowers. It was a beautiful distraction for a moment that made forming the words in his brain more difficult than it should have been.

"Oh," he said. "I see. I just—"

"My grandfather was a carpenter. My great-grandfather was a dancer."

"Oh. I'm sorry. I didn't—"

She smiled at him, easing his worries. "You didn't have any way to know. Come in. I was just making some fresh coffee. You can ask me anything you like. I don't get many visitors. And most of my friends have left the city."

He stole a quick glance at Giulia. She looked surprised and impressed that they'd earned an invitation into the woman's home so easily.

They followed Isabella inside the dimly lit foyer and she shut the door behind them, then turned back down the narrow hallway.

Sean saw the kitchen at the other end, a room that opened up to a small antique table by a window looking out over a courtyard.

He and Giulia kept their movement steady to the point of reverence. They didn't want to make any sudden moves that might startle the woman. It still surprised Sean that Isabella had allowed them into the home. Even with Giulia with him to add a certain level of trust, Sean knew that sort of thing would be unheard of in the United States, including some of the posher neighborhoods—though that depended largely on what city and state one lived in. Where he grew up in Tennessee was substantially safer than most places.

Then again, Sean wasn't as familiar with local customs in Buenos Aires. He knew crime had been rocketing skyward thanks to government corruption, hyperinflation, and lack of employment opportunities. Two of those three things were affecting the United States at the moment—the number of jobs being the only one that seemed in plentiful supply, even if few seemed interested in working.

He and Giulia passed pictures hanging from brown-painted walls, the images in the frames mostly black-and-white photos of what Sean guessed were relatives—probably long since passed. A little table sat against the wall to his left with more picture frames resting atop it. He recognized Isabella in a few of them, with who he assumed were her parents.

The wooden floor creaked under his weight as they neared the kitchen.

Isabella stood at the counter to the left. The stovetop to her right glowed bright orange. She scooped coffee out of a tin and dumped it into a percolator, then closed up the tin, set the brewing device on the stove's eye, and motioned to the table by the window.

"I have one similar to that," Giulia said, indicating the coffee pot with a nod.

Sean looked out through the window and saw that the courtyard was surrounded by a stone wall with an arched iron gate in the center. The grass was green, surrounded by a garden filled with an array of flowers.

Isabella pulled out a chair and sat down. Her guests joined her at the table, Sean taking the seat across from their hostess, Giulia the one adjacent to her.

"Do you always allow strangers into your home like this?" he asked. "It's a crazy world out there."

"I sense things about people," she said. "You're not a danger to me. You have honest eyes. And you're an attractive man. I've found most criminals around here are ugly."

Giulia shifted uncomfortably at the love fest. She rubbed her palms on her thighs to dispel the awkwardness.

Sean laughed, his cheeks burning red. "Well, thank you."

"And you're American. It isn't every day one of your people knocks on my door. Or an Italian for that matter." She cast a sidelong look over to Giulia, who smiled politely in return.

"When was the last time?" Giulia asked.

"Never."

The Italian nodded, having anticipated that response.

Sean changed directions. "You said your friends left the city. It almost sounds like you wished you could have left, too."

Her head twisted slightly, and she stared out the window at nothing in particular. "I cannot leave my family home. No matter how bad things get in the cities. It is my home. It's been in my family since my great-grandfather."

Sean understood what she meant. That was a thing people in the Old Countries did more than back home in the States. On one of his visits to Germany, he'd met a family who'd been in the same house for five hundred years. He remembered thinking the old adage "They don't build them like they used to" and truly appreciating that phrase for every ounce of its worth.

He'd marveled at how the family had been able to keep such an old building structurally sound, on top of all the other cosmetic maintenance that had to be done over the course of five centuries.

Traditions like that were long lost in the United States.

Sean considered his next words carefully, not wanting to jump straight into the point of his visit, but at the same time also reluctant to waste the woman's time.

"I am working on an investigation into the disappearance of a highly valuable item," he said.

"You mentioned that." Isabella smiled politely at him.

The percolator on the stove bubbled and hissed.

"One moment. The coffee is ready."

She stood and walked over to the stove, removed the brew from the top, and took three white mugs out of a cupboard to the left, above the counter.

As she poured the coffee into the cups, the aroma filled the room.

"Sugar and milk?" she asked.

"Please," Giulia said.

Isabella looked to Sean.

"No thank you," Sean answered. "I take it black."

She returned to the table with two cups, placing them on the surface in front of her guests.

"What is it you're looking for?" She shuffled over to the fridge and removed carton of milk, picked up a jar with sugar, and set it in front of Giulia before returning to her seat.

The woman seemed interested in her visitors' plight. That was a good sign. At least she'd listen.

Sean took a breath, and began. "In 1921, a jewel known as the Florentine Diamond disappeared."

Isabella stopped stirring her coffee, as if abruptly paralyzed by his words. "What... did you say?"

Sean immediately felt as though they'd crossed a serious line and slapped on his most apologetic face. "The Florentine Diamond. Have you heard of it?"

He knew she had; the astonished look on her face was a blatant confession—the *how did you know* in her eyes.

His host cleared her throat and resumed stirring the coffee. It was a defense mechanism, a tool she used perhaps unknowingly to shift away from the subject at hand.

"I have no diamonds here, Mr. Wyatt."

He felt the familiar tug of disappointment in his chest. It was a feeling he'd known all too well as a lifelong Atlanta Falcons fan.

"I didn't think you would," he said, even though he'd hoped—somewhat naïvely—that the woman would miraculously have the gem in her possession. "My colleague and I discovered something unusual on a replica of the diamond. It's currently on display in Florida. The fake is set in a silver stand, and your address was inscribed on the base of this sculpture, along with an interesting phrase—the dance of the stone begins."

She blinked rapidly, focusing on every detail of what he said. When he was done, she sat quietly for half a minute.

"What do you know about my great-grandfather?" Isabella asked, seeming to detour the conversation.

Sean pursed his lips together and shook his head. He lifted his hands from the coffee mug in a show of surrender. "Like I said before, not much. Nothing really. Only names."

"Same," Giulia added.

Isabella nodded, took a sip, and set her mug down just as Sean raised his and let the aromatic tendrils of steam snake their way into his nose.

He closed his eyes for a second, appreciating the delightful smell, and then took a sip.

"It's hot," she warned, a moment too late.

Sean had forgotten she'd brewed the coffee on the stove top, and as a result had produced a nearly scalding-hot liquid. Fortunately, he'd given it a little time to cool off, so it didn't burn as much as it could have.

He winced as the brew touched his lips and quickly withdrew from the mug, placing it back down on the table to resist temptation—and avoid possible injury.

Giulia snorted a laugh at his recklessness.

Isabella smiled at him and gently blew onto the surface of her coffee, dispelling the steam into the ether.

"Do you know anything about this diamond?" Sean asked, recovering from the embarrassing and somewhat painful error. "Anything at all? Based on the little research we have available, it seems he may have been the last person to come into contact with it after Charles the First of Austria."

Isabella lifted the mug to her lips and took a cautious sip. Then she set the cup down and met Sean's pleading gaze.

"My great-grandfather wondered if anyone would ever come here in search of the diamond." She glanced thoughtfully out the window again. "So did my grandfather, and my parents. No one ever did. It worried my mother to have such an item linked to our family. But my great-grandfather made sure all of us understood the importance of our role."

"Your role?" Sean walked the tightrope between pressing too much and genuine curiosity.

"Before I say anything more, I must ask, have you ever heard of a man named Clarence Gibbs?"

8

"We have," Sean answered. "Although, only recently for me."

Isabella shrugged as if it was no big deal. "Interesting. He wasn't a prominent historical figure. And he's been dead a long time."

"We know the name," Sean added. "But we don't know much about the guy. Could you give us a little more information?"

"Clarence Gibbs was a procurer of rare and valuable items after the Great War. He traveled the globe, collecting priceless heirlooms, jewels, artifacts, and artwork. No one—at least in my family—ever knew who he was, except for my great-grandfather."

"Sounds like an interesting sort." Sean had met people of that ilk before, the most recent a guy who went all over the world in search of extremely rare guitars. He was the buyer for a guitar museum in a town that also served as a music venue. His job was to locate and purchase guitars played by some of the most famous musicians in rock 'n' roll history.

Sean had seen the museum collection on a couple of occasions, both times taking the tour so he could see the impressive instruments. There was something about being in the presence of a guitar that had been strummed by such talented fingers, driven to their utmost potential by musical genius.

It was a humbling thing to behold.

One of the tour guides had explained to Sean that one of the guitars that belonged to a certain famous guitarist was seen again by the musician some forty years after he'd played it. The man was brought to tears, and as he cradled the ax again, and plugged it into an amp, it sang its notes just as beautifully as it had decades before—long-lost friends reunited once more.

Sean found himself dreaming of that kind of job, of traveling the world and simply buying priceless works of art, artifacts, or precious heirlooms. He doubted there was nearly as much gunplay with that kind of gig.

Then again, it might be a dreadful bore to do that kind of job, not to mention the people he'd have to haggle with over price and authenticity.

Maybe when he retired that kind of work might suit him better. As for now, he had plenty of gas left in the tank.

"I don't know much about Gibbs, other than the little information that was passed down by my family," Isabella continued. "He was an American, though I'm not sure what part he came from."

"It's a big country," Sean said.

"Is there anything else that you can tell us about him?"

Their hostess rolled her shoulders. "I wish there was more, but I truthfully don't know anything else. Except for one thing."

The room seemed to fill with anticipation, like a balloon ready to burst. Sean felt himself lean forward involuntarily, and even the stoic Giulia was breathless with anticipation.

Isabella raised her mug once more and held it close to her lips, concealing half her mouth before she continued.

"The only other detail I know about Mr. Gibbs was that he worked for someone very powerful, and very interested in the preservation of historical artifacts—particularly after the Great War."

Gibbs sounded like the kind of guy Tommy and Sean could use at the IAA... if he hadn't lived so long ago.

"I don't suppose you know who his employers were, do you?" Giulia ventured.

"No. According to my family, he was a secretive man."

Sean still had one more question, and even though he knew the answer wouldn't lead them to the diamond, at least it would fill in one gap in the story. "How did your great-grandfather come to know Mr. Gibbs?"

Isabella's lips spread into a smile. "Clarence Gibbs was a resourceful man, according to my mother. He knew that there would be many who would try to steal the diamond from the former emperor. So, Gibbs bought it from him a few months before Charles the First died."

Sean's jaw nearly hit the table. The coffee mug in his hand tilted almost to the point of spilling some of the hot liquid over the rim.

"What did you say?" Sean asked, his mind grasping at clarification.

"Gibbs bought the Florentine Diamond. That's how I was told it happened, anyway."

"What did he do with it?" Giulia asked. It was a loaded question, full of potential backfires. But she wanted to know. They'd flown all the way to the bottom of the planet to find out that answer.

"That... is the correct question."

The two guests waited, desperate to learn the secret.

"Gibbs knew the people who wanted the diamond would find him sooner or later, no matter how good he was at evading enemies and thieves. He also believed that the emperor himself would try to reacquire the diamond after Gibbs left the hotel where he was exiled on the island of Madeira."

Sean quickly put the pieces together. "So, Gibbs left Madeira anticipating an ambush or theft and came here to Argentina?"

"Correct."

"And he gave your great-grandfather the diamond to keep it safe," Sean finished.

"Yes. Mr. Gibbs was a trusted friend of my great-grandfather. I don't know how or why they met, but I do know that my parents claimed he was considered part of the family. I believe Gibbs helped my great-grandfather at some point, though I'm not sure in what way. I was told he was a kind man."

Giulia listened and waited for a break in the conversation before speaking. "Your great-grandfather was a dancer, yes?"

"Yes, as I mentioned before, that was his occupation, but he also had many students. He ran a dance school here in Buenos Aires."

"The dance of the stone," Sean whispered.

Isabella nodded. "I was told that someday I might meet a visitor who came asking about the diamond and mention the dance of the stone. I believe that was Mr. Gibbs' final clue to the whereabouts of the gem. It was his way of paying tribute to my great-grandfather for taking on such a dangerous charge, keeping a priceless piece of history like that safe."

"So, it was here," Giulia realized. "But not anymore."

"No. It wasn't in this place for very long. Mr. Gibbs gave my great-grandfather specific instructions for it."

"Instructions?"

Isabella took a sip of coffee then set the mug down.

Sean and Giulia watched as she reached her hands up behind her neck and fiddled with the clasp. After a few seconds it came free, and the chain drooped. She lifted it and passed it across the table, setting it in front of the two guests.

"This was what my great-grandfather left behind for the one who came searching for the dance of the stone."

Sean studied the locket. Giulia did the same, neither willing to reach out and take it to have a closer look.

"No one else has come here in the last hundred years and uttered that phrase?" the Italian asked.

"No," Isabella said, twisting her head back and forth slowly. "It would seem Mr. Gibbs hid his secret well."

Sean didn't want to be indelicate, but he had to know more. They were close, but it also felt like he was just arriving at the trailhead for wherever this was going to lead.

"The locket," he said, "what does Y P mean?"

"Yolanda Perez," Isabella answered.

Sean didn't know the name, but he'd waited as long as he thought it appropriate to pick up the locket and have a closer look. He reached across the table and pulled it toward him. Isabella nodded approvingly and continued drinking her coffee.

"Who is Yolanda Perez?" Giulia wondered.

"Yolanda was a friend of my great-grandfather. I don't believe there was anything romantic between them. If there was, my great-grandmother would not have allowed that to stay in the family."

"She must have been close," Sean noted, turning the locket over in his fingers.

"Yes. My grandparents told me that my great-grandfather saved her life when she was crossing a road here in Buenos Aires. Cars were still very new back then. She was walking across a street, and a driver didn't see her. My great-grandfather happened to be going the other way, grabbed her, and dove clear of the oncoming car, narrowly missing it. They remained friends until he died."

Giulia shifted in her seat, leaning closer to Sean to get a better look at the locket. "What happened to her?"

"Yolanda was originally from Cuba, but her home was in Miami, where she owned a bookstore. Apparently, she was visiting Buenos Aires in search of some rare books to add to her shelves. My great-grandfather maintained correspondence with her the rest of his life, even after she returned to Miami."

"Miami?" Sean lifted his gaze to look at their hostess.

"Yes."

Sean's mind spun at 5,000 rpms, but one very clear realization stood out amid the swarming thoughts. "Your great-grandfather entrusted Yolanda with the diamond."

Giulia looked up at him, startled by the abrupt and seemingly random leap to the conclusion. "What?" She turned to Isabella, who continued smiling, although with sparkling mischief in her eyes.

"Yes. As I said before, I was trusted to keep that locket, and its secret, for whoever came asking about the dance of the stone. I have no children of my own, so I feared the truth would die with me when my time comes. I could leave it with a friend, but this feels like a family matter."

Sean felt his heart beat faster, the same way it always did when clues started unraveling in front of his eyes.

"May I?" He held up the locket.

Isabella nodded and took another sip of coffee.

Sean carefully pried open the locket at the seam and unfolded it until he and Giulia could see inside.

On the right side was an address, inscribed in tiny letters and numbers. It was a locale in Miami and reminded him of the address they'd seen on the bottom of the sculpture holding the replica diamond. On the left interior side of the locket was a piece of glossy paper with a butterfly printed on it. The yellow and black wings had faded through the decades, but it was still easy enough to imagine what it might have looked like when it was first created.

"A butterfly?" Giulia questioned.

"Yolanda loved butterflies and books. That's really all I know about her as a person, other than the friendship with my great-grandfather."

"Butterflies," Sean repeated. He turned over the locket in his hand, inspecting the inscription. The address burned into his memory. "I guess this is the next place we're supposed to look."

"Yolanda has been gone a long time. I don't know what that address is for. But I'm certain she must have left a clue to the location of the diamond. It wasn't in Mr. Gibbs' plan for it to disappear forever."

"It would be nice if we knew who he worked for," Giulia mused.

Sean huffed his agreement. *That would be nice*, he thought.

He started to pass the locket back to Isabella.

"No, you can keep it," she said. "That was what my great-grandfather intended."

Sean grinned at her. "It's okay. You keep it. I have the address memorized. I wouldn't want to take something that's been in your family for over a century."

She mirrored his smile, but there was a subtle difference in her eyes. Was it appreciation, or pity? Normally, he could read people's body language and expressions with ease. It was a skill that had served him well throughout his life. Now, though, he wasn't sure.

"As I said, you are the one who is meant to have it now. I can't take it with me, after all."

Sean flashed a concerned look at her. She quickly caught the meaning.

"Oh, no," she added. "I'm not dying. Well, we're all dying. But I plan on living many more years. But you must take the locket. I insist."

He knew there was no way she was going to let him refuse. As guilty as he felt for taking a family heirloom, he understood. This was part of the game, a piece of a puzzle that had been hidden for decades. He wondered how many treasure hunters had tried to find the diamond and had the first clue right under their noses on the base of the replica. How many more people had laid eyes on her locket without knowing what was hidden inside? And even if they had, would they have known what it meant?

Doubtful.

Sean learned long ago that the best place to hide things was often in plain sight. Edgar Allen Poe had taught him that.

"Thank you," he managed, closing the locket and slipping it into a pants pocket. "I'll take good care of it."

"I know you will."

"Thank you for your help," Giulia said. "I truly appreciate it. And the coffee, which is excellent, by the way."

"You're very kind. I imagine you have very good coffee in Italy, or so I've heard."

Giulia raised a shoulder and blushed slightly. "I suppose we do okay with it."

Sean stood and raised his cup one more time, taking another long drink. "We'll leave you to your day. We've taken up enough of your time as it is."

"Oh, it's all right. I don't have much to do anyway. I was going to the market to get some fruit, and maybe read a book. Do you read much fiction?"

Sean's eyes twinkled. "Every chance I get. Although my life is sometimes much stranger than anything you'll find in novels."

The room fell silent for a second, and Sean was about to turn and head for the door when he heard a sound from that direction.

He recognized it immediately. It sounded like someone was trying to unlock the front door—without a key.

"Isabella?" Sean said, his voice suddenly urgent. "Were you expecting someone else today?"

Her smile faded only slightly, replaced by vague confusion. "No. Why?"

He faced Giulia. "Get her upstairs. Now."

"What?" Giulia wore the same confusion. Almost as if she thought he was kidding around.

"We have company. Get her upstairs. I'll handle it."

"Are you—"

"Do it."

A bump from the front door told him they were already out of time.

9

Sean clenched his jaw. He never liked being put in this kind of situation.

When he was active with Axis, and even now with the IAA, facing trouble like this was something he was built to handle. And so far, he'd come out clean on the other side. But with Giulia and Isabella in this scenario, things were much trickier.

He didn't know much about Giulia, but Sean had to assume she wasn't a trained killer. And Isabella obviously wasn't—unless he'd completely missed something.

Initially, he'd thought sending the two women upstairs was the right move, but that call changed quickly when he remembered the stairs were at the front of the house, which was way too close to the front door and the immediate threat.

Sean turned his attention back to their hostess. "Do you have another way out of this house? I mean out there?" He indicated the back yard. He'd noticed the door in the corner but wasn't sure if the outdoor area were fully enclosed.

Isabella nodded. "Yes. Through the courtyard in the back. I rarely go out that way, though—"

"That will have to do." He glanced out the windows. He didn't see anyone blocking the exit, but that didn't mean they weren't hiding behind the wall just on the other side.

"Get to the door," he ordered, "and stay on the porch. Keep down and out of sight. Do not leave unless I tell you to."

Another heavy thud shuddered the front door, testing the strength of the old wood.

Worry painted the women's faces.

"What are you going to do?" Giulia hissed, her head snapping toward the front door as it bumped again.

"Probably better if you don't know. Just get out there on the porch, stay low, and wait. Do not leave without me."

Giulia grabbed Isabella by the wrist and ushered her toward the door.

Sean watched the two women disappear outside and crouch low and out of view. He swiveled around, stepped over to the counter, and grabbed two of the knives off the magnetic strip attached to the wall.

Then another loud thud rocked the home, and this time the sound of the wooden doorframe cracking reverberated through the hall and kitchen.

Sean tucked in next to the fridge, gripping one of the knives by the blade's tip. He focused on the sounds of the men moving through the house. Without knowing how many there were, it was hard to venture a guess as to what the interlopers' strategy might be, but Sean figured at least two, and probably more. One would go up the stairs and sweep the second floor while another would remain here on the main floor and clear the area.

As expected, Sean heard the floor creak underfoot from just around the corner in the hallway.

He slowed his breath. As a result, his heart rate dipped as well to a steady, calm rhythm. Sean would have preferred to have his Springfield .40 cal with him with the prototype box suppressor attached to the end. That wasn't an option right now, so he'd have to make do with the knives.

Something squeaked overhead. It was the kind of sound a floor made under the weight of a person. Sean had been correct in figuring whoever broke in would send at least one person upstairs to snoop around.

Unfortunately, he was unable to guess how many were in the hallway mere feet from where he stood.

A faint shadow moved across the hallway wall.

Sean's grip on the knife tightened slightly.

A suppressor barrel appeared first, extended out by a pair of gloved hands.

Sean held his breath.

The man holding the gun did what he was supposed to. He checked the area directly ahead of him first, then swept his weapon to the left. It was a quick move, one that spoke to a former life in law enforcement or perhaps the military.

But it wasn't quick enough.

As he spun left, Sean's arm was already in motion. By the time the man realized the danger, it was too late. The knife sank into his left eye before he could fire a shot.

The gunman staggered as his consciousness was severed from his body, and then he slumped against the wall, sliding down to the floor in a heap.

Sean heard the next threat react from a few steps behind the first guy. He knew the second would be more careful.

He flung open the refrigerator door just as the second gunman whipped around the corner and fired.

Rounds plunked into the door but didn't puncture it.

Sean stayed low behind the door and then leaned out, flicking the next blade at the shooter.

This throw was less calculated and sailed wildly at the gunman. Still, it was flung with enough force that when the base of the hilt hit the guy in the head, it dazed him for a second, and he stepped back.

Sean sprang from his cover and charged the gunman.

The shooter reacted, regaining his composure enough to raise the weapon once more. Sean grabbed the suppressor before the guy could get off another shot. He jerked the gun to his right, then twisted it up and back toward the assailant.

The man winced but jabbed at Sean's face with his left hand. It was a pathetic effort, and while it would have probably been good enough in a street fight with most of the hoodlums out there, it was a simple punch to dodge for Sean Wyatt.

The man's trigger finger snapped as Sean continued to twist the pistol. He yelped in pain and instinctively let go, immediately on the offensive with his good hand. He launched another punch, this one more accurate and faster than the first. Still, the gloved fist merely glanced off Sean's cheek as he turned the pistol upside down and fired with his pinky finger on the trigger.

The muzzle clicked and puffed, sending a round into the man's chest. Sean twisted the weapon up slightly, and twitched the trigger a second time. The bullet went through the man's neck and out the top of his head, painting the wall behind him in an abstract crimson.

He slumped to the floor with his back hitting the wall on the way down. Sean doubted the guy upstairs heard the innocuous, muted gunshot. But he may have heard the bodies hitting the floor.

A quick check toward the back of the house produced no sign of the women. That was what he'd hoped, for them to be out of sight. And for the moment, no attackers were creeping across the courtyard or over the wall in the back.

Both good signs.

He heard the ceiling creak overhead. The guy upstairs was moving around. Something thudded and crashed.

He's tearing up the place, Sean thought. The idea of these goons wrecking this woman's house dumped jet fuel on the anger burning in his chest.

Sean quickly took the pistol from the other dead man and moved down the hall to the base of the stairs.

The door hung slightly ajar. He wedged his foot against it in case there was another assassin lurking just beyond, covering the exit, then aimed his pistol up the stairs. He didn't see anyone yet, but the sounds of a room being ransacked continued to echo down the stairwell—now clearer than when he was in the kitchen.

Sean spun quickly and poked the weapon through the gap

between the door and the splintered doorframe. No one stood in the doorway, so he immediately and quietly shut the door before returning his attention up the stairs.

He crept up the first couple of steps with the pistols in his hands pointed to the landing ahead. When he was halfway up, he twisted his left arm, aiming the gun in that hand toward an open door on the second floor.

Sean kept ascending, using the balls of his feet to step on the edges of the stairs to prevent any sounds from the old boards.

The man upstairs—he assumed it was only one—wasn't taking anywhere near the care to keep quiet. And the higher Sean climbed, the louder the sounds grew.

There were two rooms upstairs and a bathroom at the end of the hall, where Sean paused for a second to check inside and make sure no one was there. He found it empty and crept forward along the wall, staying close to the baseboards—again to prevent his weight from pushing down too much on the center of the floor and causing an alarming squeak.

Sean believed he had the element of surprise. And that was the greatest advantage you could get in a situation like this.

He slowed down when he neared the first bedroom door on the right, holding the pistol up high, close to the external part of the frame.

The sound of glass breaking escaped from the next door. Still, he leaned forward and aimed the pistol through the open door next to him and swept the area in a single second.

Clear.

It was possible more than one of these goons had come up the stairs and were setting an ambush for him—perhaps from the closet across from the bed. But he ruled that out. The room had already been roughed up. The navy-blue linens with a seafoam-green comforter were tossed on the floor, the mattress cut in multiple places. Nightstands were turned over, and the dresser drawers littered the floor.

The closet doors had been opened but only partially closed, so if there was a person hiding in there, they'd have to really squeeze into the shadows.

Sean glanced down the stairwell one more time, then focused on the last door at the end of the hallway on the left, where the sounds came from.

He inched forward, picking his way along the floor, hoping he wouldn't step on a soft spot in the wood that would alert the enemy to his presence.

Sean managed to reach the near corner of the doorway without more than a rustle of the air.

He craned his neck and peeked into the room. Straight ahead the master bed was a disaster. The floral comforter and light blue sheets had been ripped off, and the mattress cut up with multiple gashes in haphazard patterns across it.

Stepping around the doorframe, Sean leveled the pistol and stepped in. The closet door in the back-right corner hung open, with clothes strewn about on the floor.

An antique dresser sat in the middle of the floor against the far wall between the closet door and the door to the master bathroom. Drawers had been pulled out and tossed on the floor, along with their contents of underwear, socks, and shirts.

Sean found the thug responsible in the master bathroom, jerking out a vanity drawer and sifting through them before moving on to the next.

Lining up the pistol's sights with the man's left shoulder, Sean tensed his trigger finger. "Don't move," he ordered.

The gunman in the bathroom snapped his head around to see the American standing in the doorway with a pistol trained on him—a pistol that looked an awful lot like the one in his right hand.

He was halfway bent over with his left hand on a drawer handle. It was a compromising position, and one that gave him virtually no chance to get off a shot before taking a bullet in the shoulder, or worse—the neck or head.

"Your buddies downstairs are dead. What you do next will decide whether you're going to join them now, or later."

The man said nothing, and it wasn't clear whether or not he understood Sean. Because he was hunched over, it was hard to tell how tall the guy was, but Sean guessed a few inches shorter than him, but with broad shoulders like a rugby player.

His dark, nearly black hair was pulled up in a man bun, and he peered back at Sean with eyes that nearly matched the bluish gray of Sean's.

For what it was worth, the assassin obeyed Sean's order to not move, though it was easy to see that was primarily due to his brain trying to figure a way out of this mess.

"If you want to live," Sean said, "put the gun down. And tell me who you work for."

The man stood at an uncomfortable angle, hunched over the white antique vanity. He couldn't stay in that position for long before his lower back started aching—or maybe that was something that didn't happen until the mid-forties.

Sean tried to recall, but there were so many more painful moments in his life—such as being shot, stabbed, punched, kicked, and myriad other things.

"There's no way out of here," Sean promised him. "We have the exits covered. You and your friends walked into a trap."

The look in the assassin's eyes wasn't a promising one. He bore the expression of a cornered badger, with fearless, angry eyes and a grimly set jaw. His lips remained pressed together in firm resolve.

Before the guy even twitched, Sean knew exactly how this was going to go down. This was a man who had no intention of being taken alive.

The burglar's right arm abruptly moved in an attempt to raise and aim his weapon, but it didn't even get halfway up.

Sean fired the pistol in his right hand, keeping the other low by his side. He only needed one round for this, and it struck true right in the meat of the man's right arm. The sidearm in the guy's hand fired a single shot down into the corner of the wall before it fell from his fingers, nerves and muscles instantly damaged from the wound.

He grunted, dropped to one knee, and glowered at the American.

Smoke trailed out of the muzzle, filling the air with the bitter scent of spent powder—a stark contrast to the flowery potpourri Isabella kept in the room.

The man grimaced, and his breathing intensified as the burning pain from the bullet and the torn tissue started pulsing into his brain.

"You're a dead man," the assassin threatened.

"If I had a euro for every time someone said that to me," Sean drawled. "Make this easy on yourself. You don't have to die here. Tell me who you work for. Who sent you?"

The guy shook his head. A disturbing grin teased across his lips, baring pearly white teeth. "You have no idea what you've done. You just put a target on your back."

Sean shook his head slowly. "I don't know if you realize it, but you just checked off every box in the bad guy's big book of clichés. You ransacked this woman's place. So overdone. Check. Then you threaten me by telling me I'm a dead man, which I've heard more times than I can count. Check. Now you continue to offer vague threats in hopes that by stalling me, one of your other guys can rush up here and save the day. Check. Highly unimaginative if you ask me."

The man's right cheek twitched just beneath his eye.

"So, let's just skip all of that, and you tell me what you're doing here and who you—"

Before Sean could finish, the man's left hand dove toward the pistol. His fingers brushed against the grip as he desperately tried to snatch it. Sean didn't hesitate. He had no choice.

He squeezed the trigger on the pistol and sent a round through the front corner of the man's head.

The thug fell over on his side and never moved again.

Sean breathed calmly and lowered the pistol to his side like the other. Hazy gray smoke hung around him, filling his nostrils with the acrid smell.

He remained still for a few seconds, listening closely for any sign that another killer might be sneaking up behind him. He glanced back over his shoulder and saw nothing, and heard the same.

He needed to make sure the two women downstairs were all right. So, Sean turned and hurried out of the room and down the stairs.

When he reached the base of the staircase, he twisted the deadbolt into its housing to secure the front door again, thankful for the moment that the intruders hadn't damaged it along with the main bolt.

There'd been no one outside waiting to ambush him before, perhaps sneak in while his back was turned, but that didn't mean reinforcements weren't out there.

He moved quickly back down the hall to the kitchen, stepped over the bodies of the other two guys, and stepped over to the back door, where he paused and looked out across the courtyard. Standing in this spot, he saw Giulia and Isabella crouched down just behind the walls near the window.

Sean didn't see anyone else in the yard, or beyond it.

He opened the door, which startled both women. Their surprise turned to relief when they saw it was Sean.

"You okay?" he asked.

The two women looked at each other, then to him, both nodding.

"Yes," Isabella answered. "What happened?"

Sean saw her eyes fall to the pistols in his hands, and he hurriedly tucked one into the back of his belt.

He was about to tell them not to look in through the window, but it was too late. Giulia and their host turned and stared through the window at the carnage inside.

Isabella covered her mouth, breath caught in her throat as she gazed in horror at the two bodies.

Giulia wrapped her arm around the woman, but it was obvious the scene shoved a spike of discomfort through her gut.

Sean went into protection mode. "Ms. Fernandez," he said, grabbing her softly by the shoulders, "is there somewhere you can go? Somewhere safe? Just for a few days? Maybe one of those friends you mentioned who moved out of the city?"

The palm covering her mouth dropped away, and she looked at

him. Confusion filled her eyes, giving off the appearance of being completely lost.

Somehow, she managed to nod her head. "Yes. Yes, I have somewhere I can go."

"Good." He turned to Giulia. "Call the police. After they arrive, she can go upstairs and collect whatever she needs to take with her out of town."

"Yes. Okay," Giulia said.

"I have another call I need to make while you do that." Sean took out his phone and thumbed through the contact list until he found Emily Starks.

Giulia was a little slower getting her phone. She was too busy staring in rapt bewilderment at Sean Wyatt. Isabella's gaze was locked on him as well.

"What kind of archaeologist are you?" their hostess asked.

Sean pressed the phone to his ear and heard it start ringing. "Not the kind you see on the History Channel."

10

Totti steamed from an alcove across the street where he'd parked the car. It was shaded by the building next to it, making the vehicle a little less visible to anyone who might have looked out of the home.

He'd seen Giulia Agosti go in the building with a man he'd come to learn was Sean Wyatt. The American had a particularly unusual career working for the International Archaeological Agency. With some digging, Totti had learned the man always seemed to escape legal trouble even when he found himself in deep.

There were several killings linked to the man, all in self-defense —of course. Totti initially rolled his eyes at the thought. A single defensive killing was rare enough, but for someone to have more than one was preposterous. That meant Wyatt had some kind of pull, probably at a high government level.

What Totti couldn't figure out was what Wyatt had done before he started working for the IAA. His record was oddly blank between the time he graduated and the time he joined the archaeological agency in Atlanta.

There were plenty of people with that sort of background. He might have taken some years to go travel the world, or worked in an anonymous job somewhere. If he'd been a bartender or carpenter, ranch hand, landscaper, none of those things would have come up on Totti's searches.

But those possible explanations didn't jibe with the man's exploits as a so-called archaeologist.

There was something more to this Sean Wyatt. Totti simply couldn't put his finger on it what it could be.

Typically, signals such as these pointed to government work, or perhaps paramilitary, special ops, or mercenary employment. For all Totti knew, it might be every one of those things.

Still, it shouldn't have been a problem for the three men he sent inside the Fernandez house.

They were all killers to their core, each with more than a few notches on their belts for the lives they'd taken. Lorenzo Rossi didn't accept just anyone into his organization. You had to prove yourself worthy. And the payment was always in blood taken.

All this caused a rare splinter of worry to work its way into Totti's mind. His men had been inside the house for more than ten minutes. He'd told himself he would give them fifteen, but after they'd barged through the front door, it really should have taken fewer than five to get the woman, and anything she might have in the house related to the location of the diamond, if not the gem itself.

A few minutes after his men entered the home, the front door closed again.

Totti thought that was odd, but he figured one of his men must have done it to prevent any random passersby from getting suspicious about a door hanging open. Just as bad, a friend of Fernandez might walk by, think the woman was coming out, and stand there to wait for her, perhaps to strike up a conversation. Eventually, that person would push the door open and find out what was going on inside.

He imagined his men were pressing the woman for information, at least initially. But as the seconds ticked by, Totti's concern grew.

Finally, out of impatience, he spoke into the microphone on his radio.

"One, what is taking so long?"

Totti waited, but no response came.

"One, come in. What's your status? Do you have the woman?"

Instead of hearing the team leader he'd sent in, the faint sound of sirens whined from somewhere down the street. They were still far enough away for him to get out of position, but surely the cops weren't coming here to the Fernandez house.

They must have been rushing to some other incident.

Even as he told himself that, Totti had a bad feeling that wasn't the case.

Something was wrong, and there was no way he could risk getting out of the car, running across the street, and going into the home.

He exhaled deeply, shifted the vehicle into drive, and drove out of the shadows and onto the street.

Totti wasn't going to go far. Just half a block down to get clear of the house, just in case.

"I'm moving down the street," he said into the radio.

Why aren't they responding? The question plagued him as he pulled into a spot on the curb between two compact cars.

From here, he could watch the front of the house through the rearview mirror, and the position would allow him an easy getaway if the cops really were coming to this location.

The screams of the sirens swelled, and the buildings around him seemed to amplify the annoying sound.

A police car zoomed around the corner ahead, forcing two other vehicles to pull off on the side of the road.

The cop sped to the front of the Fernandez house, where he stopped abruptly and jumped out of the vehicle.

Not good, Totti thought.

More sirens filled the air in the usually quiet neighborhood. People on the sidewalks turned and looked as three additional police cars flooded the scene. Two came from the other direction and blocked the street behind Totti, just beyond where he'd been parked only a moment before.

The other did the same only twenty meters behind where he currently sat.

He knew he needed to get out of there. Abandoning his men wasn't an option. Not usually. But they were done for now.

It wasn't as if he could jump out of his car and start picking off the cops. There were too many witnesses standing around watching the scene play out.

"Get out of there now," Totti ordered into the radio. But he knew it was in vain.

There was only one reason none of his three men would answer him. Even if they were torturing the people inside the house, one of them would have answered. That meant all three of them were dead, or worst-case scenario; unconscious.

He doubted that, but the paranoid part of him did wonder. If the men were still alive, they could talk. And no one talked about the Rossi Clan.

As far as he knew, only a scant few members of the organization had ever squealed on the family. And those men had died gruesome, torturous deaths.

A single question in Totti's mind was how they'd been taken down by the American and the two women.

Perhaps there was more to this Wyatt, as he initially suspected.

It certainly wasn't the Italian archaeologist. Her dossier was easier to read than a children's book. Good grades in school, college, graduate degree in archeology. Rented an apartment. Paid her taxes.

It wasn't compelling reading.

With this Wyatt, however, Totti felt like maybe he'd found a challenge. The idea excited him slightly. He hadn't run into a problem that needed solving in a while, and when it had happened in the past, it was easily dealt with.

Perhaps Wyatt would be a worthy adversary. And Totti would relish killing him, especially to avenge the deaths of his men.

He glanced in the rearview mirror again, watching the cops go up to the front door and knock. Then he shifted the car into gear and accelerated away slowly, passing another police car as it whipped around the curve, en route to the crime scene.

It didn't look like the cops had paid him any notice. That was the only victory Totti would take from this failed operation. And he knew Lorenzo Rossi would not be pleased with the results.

The only way he was going to avoid catching the boss's wrath was to make sure it didn't happen again.

He took out his phone as he slowed to a stop at a red light and looked up the name of one of his most trusted henchmen—Vincenzo Bartolo.

Totti pressed the green button and raised the device to his ear.

"What kind of trouble did you run into this time, Barone?" the man asked. His tone was every bit as gruff as the guy himself.

"I don't know."

Silence followed the response.

"Interesting."

Totti knew his honest response would catch the man by surprise, and not because he was telling the truth. Bartolo was well aware of Totti's methods and his skillset. Bartolo was a problem solver, too—a brutal one.

"Who's the mark?" the man grumbled.

Totti grinned. "An American named Sean Wyatt. And I want you find out everything you can about him."

11

Sean waited in a chair in the kitchen as the police sirens zoomed in on the street in front of Isabella Fernandez's house.

He'd told the two women to go upstairs and start collecting some necessities for Isabella to take to a friend's house, and when they were done, they had returned downstairs and were now out on the back porch.

Sitting in a room with a couple of dead bodies wasn't the kind of thing most ordinary people could handle. He could only imagine the horror the women must have felt, first stepping over the bodies here in the kitchen and then seeing the one upstairs.

Sean hadn't so much as covered them, which he figured might have been helpful in hindsight. But this was a crime scene, and the fewer things he tampered with—particularly around the bodies—the better.

He'd spoken to Emily Starks who, he guessed, had already gotten in contact with the Buenos Aires police department to let them know what really happened, and that her former agent had acted in self-defense.

So far in his life after Axis, her phone calls had dragged him out of more than a few sticky situations.

As the director of one of the most secretive agencies in the world, Emily Starks had some serious pull, and even Sean didn't always know how or why.

He heard doors slamming outside the house and glanced back out through one of the rear windows to make sure the two women were still okay.

They sat on a couple of patio chairs, both looking extremely nervous.

Sean waited, a cup of coffee sitting next to where his elbow rested on the table.

Several hard knocks at the door signaled the cops were there.

"Enter!" he shouted in Spanish.

He'd unlocked it before returning to the kitchen and pouring himself another coffee, and within a second of giving the command, the men in uniform poured into the house.

As expected, their weapons were trained on him almost instantly as they pushed ahead through the hallway.

Sean kept his hands where the police could see them and remained almost perfectly still.

"Stay right there," the lead cop ordered. He looked young, probably mid-twenties, but Sean guessed the man had already seen more than a few bodies in this town.

Sean waited until the man spoke to him again. "Where is the gun?" the cop asked.

The question was expected. Sean first answered the man with his eyes—a quick look over to the kitchen counter next to the sink. "There are three on that counter," Sean answered in fluid Spanish. "All belonged to the dead men."

The cop followed his eyes to the pistols sitting on the bar. Three other men in uniform entered the building, all hanging back behind the first.

"Check upstairs," he said to no one in particular. It was the kind of order he expected to be followed by at least one of the men. The man in the back turned and scurried up the stairs, keeping his pistol aimed high as he climbed.

"What happened here?" the first cop asked. He didn't lower his weapon. Fortunately, Sean had grown accustomed to having a gun pointed at him. It wasn't the kind of thing he wanted to be used to, but that party boat had sailed long ago.

"My colleague and I came here to see the homeowner, Isabella Fernandez. They're both outside on the porch. I thought it best if they didn't stay in the room with a couple of corpses. Fernandez has a small suitcase of items she'll need. I thought it best she find a safe place to stay outside the city for a while."

He paused before resuming the story. "Three men—your guy upstairs will find the third—broke into the house. Fortunately, the front door is sturdy. They barged in, and the only thing that kept us all from being killed was that it could take a beating long enough for the two women to get out onto the patio."

The cop studied Sean, trying to judge whether or not the American was telling the truth.

"Anyone else in the house?" the younger man asked.

"No, sir."

The policeman seemed to accept the answer. This was reinforced when he finally lowered his weapon—something Sean figured he would not have done had they not received a call from a certain clandestine agency director.

Sean continued the story about what happened as the cop stepped closer to the body with the knife sticking out of it. It was a grisly thing to behold, for any officer from a young cop to the most seasoned veteran.

"He was the first one in," Sean said. "I worked with what I had. When he appeared, I threw the knife before he could fire."

"Impressive," the cop said with a macabre, appreciative tone.

"I missed with the second guy. Had to wrestle his gun away from him, then shot him with it. After that, I went upstairs and took out the third guy, which I'm sure your partner is probably finding right about now."

"José!" a shout came from above almost as if on cue. "There's another one up here."

The leader, whose name Sean surmised must be Jose, shouted back. "Anyone else?"

"No. It's clear."

"That last one wouldn't be self-defense," Sean offered. "More like prevention."

The cop nodded that he understood, and even offered a cynical grin.

"Do you know who these men are?"

Sean didn't know for sure, but he had inspected the two bodies on the floor in the kitchen, checking for any identification. Neither of the men had anything of that sort on their person. Each had a few hundred euros in their pocket, which told Sean they weren't local, though he put those at long odds anyway.

But what really caught his attention was the tattoos on each of the three men. The marking was a black circle with a matching R in the center, done in a sort of calligraphy.

"I don't," Sean said, answering the cop's question. "Take a look at their right wrist. They all have the same tattoo. Any idea what it means?"

He waited while the two cops behind Jose bent down and took a closer look at the dead men's wrists.

"Recognize that?" Sean asked.

The men shook their heads.

"You have any weapons on you?" Officer Jose asked.

Sean shook his head. He briefly considered making a joke about his hands being deadly weapons, but thought that would be poorly timed. Also, it wasn't a joke.

"No, sir. And I took the magazines out of those on the counter." He changed subjects rapidly, feeling a pressing need to tend to Ms. Fernandez's safety. "The homeowner will need an escort to her friend's home—if it isn't too much trouble. I'm sure the investigation will take time, and you'll want to ask more questions of her and of Ms. Agosti. I don't know if there are more of these men out there, and it might be dangerous for her to go on her own. I'm also not sure if these guys were after me, and I simply brought her into the crossfire. I would rather split up, and draw any other danger away from her if at all possible."

The cop listened and when Sean was done, nodded. "You won't need to stay for further questioning Mr. Wyatt. It seems you have very important, very persuasive friends. We will provide safe travel for Ms. Fernandez. As for you and your colleague, you're free to go."

Sean said a silent thank you to Emily for the aid in getting out of this pickle, then thanked the cop.

He stood slowly, just to make sure he didn't startle the officer, and then walked over to the back door and opened it.

The two women looked over at him, a combination of fear and confusion brimmed in their eyes.

"Isabella, you're safe now. The police are here and are going to take you wherever you need to go. Giulia, you and I should go. We need to put as much distance between us and her as possible. If you want to go back to Italy, I understand. I can keep going with the investigation and let you know what I find if—"

"You're trying to get rid of me?" Giulia asked.

Sean stumbled over his answer. "No. I just—"

"I'm coming with you. That is nonnegotiable. This is the closest anyone has ever been to uncovering the location of the Florentine Diamond, and I am not going to bow out now."

Sean appreciated her courage, though he wasn't sure she fully understood the danger. Whoever sent these assassins would not be pleased their men had been killed. In his experience, that only made things worse.

"If they find us again, there will probably be more of them," Sean said.

Her burning stare never wavered. "Then I guess we need to stay one step ahead."

Sean looked back to Isabella. She seemed to have calmed down, particularly now that the police were there. He still felt guilty for bringing this kind of trouble into her home. But it could have been so much worse, and there were no guarantees that the dead men wouldn't have found her on their own.

"Thank you for your help," he offered. "I am sorry for all of this."

She managed a feeble smile and shook her head. "You saved my life. I will always be in your debt for that."

Sean dismissed the notion as Giulia stood.

"You'll be all right?" the Italian asked.

Isabella nodded.

They'd only been in Buenos Aires for a matter of hours, and now it seemed they were already leaving. If Giulia had wanted to take in some of the sights, it would have to wait for another trip.

For now, they were heading back to the States, and the only direction they had was a name and a locket. He felt the necklace in his pocket and repeated the name in his mind. *Yolanda Perez.*

Isabella said the woman had owned a bookstore. It was unlikely the shop was still around, but it was the best place to begin, along with the name. He just hoped whoever sent the dead men wasn't able to track him on the next leg of the journey.

Sean had no misgivings about that. He'd have to assume those hunting for the diamond would be right behind him, which meant he'd have to be ready.

12

"Find anything?" Giulia asked. She sat across from Sean in the IAA Gulfstream jet, a cup of coffee sitting in the cup holder to her left.

"Yolanda's obituary from 1982." Sean said. "This says the name of her bookstore was The Hidden Gem." He lifted his eyes to meet Giulia's gaze. "A little on the nose if you ask me."

"A secret message in plain sight," Giulia said, the realization hitting her immediately.

Sean nodded.

"Anything else?" she asked.

He drew a breath and exhaled. "Not much. From what I can tell, her grandkids run the store now."

"So, it's still open. That's good."

"Yes, but it doesn't get us very far. What are we supposed to do, walk in and tell them we're there to find out about a priceless diamond that their abuela secreted into the States and kept hidden for safekeeping?"

Giulia scowled at the comment. "That's what we just did in Buenos Aires. What's the hesitation now?"

Sean didn't answer right away. But he knew why. For more than a decade since he left Axis, he'd put himself in harm's way. And more often than not, others as well. It was fine for him to jump into the line of fire, to dance with the devil in the pale moonlight—he smirked at the Joker's reference from *Batman*. But there was nothing funny about his concerns.

People had been hurt, sometimes killed, because of his involvement in investigations exactly like this one. He justified it when he fell asleep at night, and when he woke every morning. He told himself that if he hadn't been involved with all those cases, many more innocent lives would have been lost or ruined.

But the pages of that old story were wearing thin, the ink fading as if spread over too many pages in time.

Now, Sean wasn't so sure. Not anymore.

Giulia's stare pierced him and shook the usually strong will of Sean Wyatt.

He got up and stretched his arms out, then paced over to the bar just behind him. There, he planted his hands on the counter and leaned into it, stretching his calf muscles.

"Whenever I get involved in something like this, people get hurt," he said. He thought the confession might make him feel better, but it had the opposite effect. It twisted in his gut like a rusty sword.

Giulia crossed one leg over the other and folded her hands atop her knee. It was a pose not unlike a therapist might take in a session, but there was no couch for him to lie back on, and Giulia wasn't in the mental health field. She was a student of history and cultures.

"So, you blame yourself for some bad things that happened in the past. Everyone carries those kinds of regrets."

He shook his head, a grim resolve setting his jaw firm. "No. Not like me. People die because of me. Because of what I do. We were lucky with Isabella back there. The only thing that kept her from being on a coroner's slab right this minute was the fact that her front door was able to absorb enough blows from the intruders for the two of you to get outside so I could…."

"So you could protect us."

He nodded, but he didn't like the answer. Even if it was right.

"Sean, Isabella would be dead right now if you weren't there. I would probably still be in Italy, doing whatever research fell in my lap."

"At least you wouldn't be in danger," he muttered.

"You don't know that." She cut herself off before saying more.

Sean turned his head and looked at her. An epiphany darkened his eyes. "What?"

Giulia looked frazzled and shifted her eyes away for a second, unwilling to face the silent judgment.

"Nothing."

"No. Why did you say that? Why wouldn't you be safe if you were back in Italy, or even Orlando for that matter?"

She straightened her jacket in an attempt to stall, or maybe come up with an explanation. But there was no getting around it. Giulia knew she had to come clean, and Sean could see it in her body language.

"I think the Rossi Clan was following me." She waited for him to yell at her, or get some kind of rebuke. Instead, she received silence, which was in some ways far worse.

"Why would you think that?" he asked after a long, deliberating pause.

Giulia visibly tried to relax. "They approached me in Italy. Some of Rossi's men asked me about the diamond. They wanted to know what I knew about it."

"And what did you tell them?"

"That the diamond was lost, that all the trails I followed turned out to be dead ends."

"How did they know you were working on locating the diamond?" The question was blunt, but Sean didn't feel like beating around the bush. He almost never did.

She swallowed, still clearly afraid of his judging stare. "It was no secret that I was trying to find the Florentine Diamond. I didn't try to hide it. Not at first. People have been searching for it for decades with no success. I shouldn't have been on anyone's radar. I guess they noticed me because I have a good reputation in my field. I am not a 'treasure hunter.' And as someone who approaches history and archaeology in a very pragmatic way, I suppose that may have worked against me in drawing the Rossi Clan's attention."

Sean listened, and everything made sense. He didn't appreciate the way she'd looked at him when she used the term *treasure hunter*, but he let it slide off his shoulders. In certain circles, the IAA definitely carried that kind of criticism. But those within the agency knew that wasn't the case.

They didn't do it for fame or money or glory. It was about preservation. They just happened to do it in unconventional ways.

It wasn't as if the IAA didn't operate in some of the usual manners, some of the standard protocols. There were several archaeologists on staff who, even at that very moment, were overseeing dig sites around the world.

But that wasn't Sean's gig. He was in charge of recovery and security. And in a world of bad people with even worse intentions, that job sometimes got dangerous.

"You said they approached you," Sean said. "And that you told them everything you'd done resulted in dead ends." It wasn't a question.

"Yes," she confirmed. "I told them nothing."

"Nothing about the replica? The one we saw in Orlando?"

"Nothing. If I had told them that, they would have inspected it before us. Or stolen it. They may not have been able to decipher its meaning. But there would have been signs of their presence. I can assure you of that."

Sean didn't know much about the Rossi Clan, and there were few if any useful resources online about them—as one would expect from trying to find information about an organized crime syndicate. Those weren't the types to leave loose ends lying around. There was more information out there about some secret societies than these people.

"I guess they didn't believe you," he said. "That's why they followed you."

She nodded. "Yes. It would seem so. They must have tailed me to

Orlando and then to Buenos Aires. But now they won't know where we're going."

Sean stood up straight and slapped on a dubious expression. "I wouldn't be so sure about that."

"What do you mean?" Worry splashed on her face—the kind that she tried to hide under a mask of false confidence. "You killed those men."

"They weren't the only ones."

"What? How do you know that?" Fear started gripping her facial features. Her cheeks paled. Her jaw tightened. He knew she clenched her teeth just behind those full, rosy lips.

"For starters, teams like that always have a handler, someone who knows where they are and what they're doing. Sort of like a puppet master calling all the shots. Those guys in Isabella's home were just the tools. They weren't the craftsmen. Second, it's possible they are tracking your phone or one of your other devices." He nodded with a look at her phone sitting on the seat next to her, plugged into a USB port. "You haven't noticed anything unusual going on with your devices, have you?"

Puzzled, she glanced over at the phone. "No. Not that I have noticed. And no one else has touched my phone, my computer, tablet, nothing."

"All your accounts are secure? Email? Social media? All that?"

Giulia shrugged, looking a little less assured about that answer. "Yes. I change my passwords regularly, and I don't use simple ones, or the ones that the computer recommends."

She was ahead of the game in that regard. Sean knew plenty of people who didn't think stuff like that was important. And that kind of thinking made things so much easier for hackers.

For the time being, he wasn't ready to question her tech security further. It was more reasonable to think that someone had followed her to Orlando, then to Buenos Aires. And that someone was still out there.

It was futile to try to think of who it could be—the handler who'd sent the death squad into Isabella Fernadez's home. But they would reveal themselves sooner or later. Waiting for that to happen would require patience, planning, and caution. Whoever was giving the orders for the Rossi Clan was willing to do whatever it took to find the diamond.

Sean wondered if whoever had tailed them to Argentina was right behind them at that moment, on another plane en route to Miami. There was no way he could know that.

For now, tens of thousands of feet in the air, they were safe. For now.

"When we arrive in Miami, we'll need to take extra care," Sean said. "I'll rent a car. And you rent one. We can book an Uber, too. I'll arrange for multiple hotel rooms under different names. Anything that can throw them off our scent. Those types find a way to check all that stuff. Hopefully, that will be enough to keep them at bay for a while."

"And if it isn't?"

"Then I'll have to handle it." He didn't sound thrilled at the idea.

She leaned forward. Her eyelids narrowed, conveying deep sincerity. "I don't know all your exploits, Sean. If it's anything like what I saw back there in Argentina, I'd say the world is a better place because of you. And if I were a person bent on some kind of evil plans, I would be very afraid."

Sean took a deep breath and sighed. He wasn't sure he necessarily wanted people to be afraid of him, but if they were aligned with dark intentions, he'd take it.

"I'm going to see if I can take a nap," he said. "You might want to do the same. All this jetting around can be exhausting. And I don't know what's waiting for us in Miami. Or where that will lead."

13

"Miami," Totti said into the phone.

"You're sure?" Vincenzo Bartolo asked.

"Of course I'm sure. I wouldn't say it if I wasn't. They are heading to Miami now. I'm close behind them. I have a team waiting to intercept them when they arrive. This Wyatt will slip up—perhaps rent a car or a hotel room. That's where I need you to alert my men on the ground so we'll know what they're up to."

"Okay. Fine. I can do that. I'll need phone numbers for your team."

"You'll have them as soon as we end this call."

Bartolo didn't say anything for a few seconds, and Totti guessed the man was trying to decide whether or not to ask something.

"This team in Miami... Are they as competent as your men were in Argentina?"

Totti's temper sent a fire through his chest that ended up in his forehead. Bartolo was on his side. But Totti wasn't inclined to take insults or those kinds of insinuations lying down.

"The men in Buenos Aires weren't at fault for what happened. The intel I had on the situation was inadequate."

"And whose fault was that?" Bartolo asked.

"I do not waste time trying to blame others for errors. Even when it costs me valuable resources." He knew he didn't have to clarify the word *resources* for Bartolo. The man knew exactly what that meant. The men under them were resources, tools for a job. And they were expendable.

That didn't mean the organization was careless with their manpower. Quite the contrary. These were more than mere mercenaries. The team members Totti lost in Buenos Aires were all loyal to their boss, Lorenzo Rossi. Every one of them would have taken a bullet for the man, and in this instance had done so even if indirectly.

Totti took it personally that he'd lost three men in what should have been an exceedingly simple raid on a woman's house. Bartolo was just as much a part of the same hierarchy, and he knew how it all worked.

"I wasn't accusing you of anything, old friend. Just trying to understand the situation so we can prevent it going forward. It would be a shame to lose more men in such a needless way."

"I agree. Which is why I called you in the first place. You are careful, meticulous, calculating. I want to make sure this sort of thing doesn't happen again."

"Understood."

Totti inclined his head and stared down the empty aisle of the private jet. It was mostly dark inside except for the single light he'd turned on overhead. He preferred it that way. It helped him focus. Too many distractions were a detriment, and he didn't want to miss a single detail for the task at hand.

He changed subjects in a heartbeat. "Were you able to find anything about Sean Wyatt?"

Bartolo cleared his throat, and right away Totti knew the response would be less than satisfying.

"Not much. Probably nothing you didn't already know. His exploits with the IAA are well documented. His past is what seems so strange. Looks intentionally covered up."

"Were you able to uncover it?"

"No. That tells me he wasn't simply off the grid for a number of years. I would guess he was involved with some kind of clandestine operation. Which one, I have no idea. CIA? Maybe. But I would guess it's something else."

Totti knew what he meant. There were government agencies that operated off the books, and they answered to only a handful of people. The names of these redacted organizations were unknown to anyone outside them. Even though they were funded by governments, the bills that provided them with what they needed always had blacked out lines of text, usually replaced with vague, innocuous terms that no politician—or their interns reading the paperwork—would think to question.

Unfortunately, there was no way to access rosters of such agencies. Names were often changed anyway, the agents operating under aliases.

There'd been leaks of CIA operatives in certain theaters on a few occasions. There was even an action movie or two about such a thing. But the names of more secretive organizations would never be revealed. Because they were already erased.

That meant Totti was flying blind—at the moment, quite literally—into the next phase of the operation. He'd have preferred to have better intel, but simply knowing that both he and Bartolo had been unable to source any information about Wyatt was enough to assume that the man was extremely dangerous, and dealing with him would require caution.

No more barging into houses.

Vermin like this were venomous, dangerous to handle. Only swift, calculated force could remove the problem.

"I'll need six more men on the ground in Miami in addition to the three I already have there."

"What?" Bartolo blurted. "Do we have—"

"Yes. Get them there. I don't care if they have to come from Italy."

"If that's the case, they will arrive after you, more than likely."

"Fine. Just get them. I don't want to take any chances. This Wyatt is more of a problem than I think either of us realize. Best we work forward from there."

"Whatever you say. I'll see what I can do." Bartolo hesitated. "Have you told Lorenzo about this yet?"

Totti hadn't made that call. He wanted to make sure everything was lined up to prevent another disaster. "No. I will fill him in on the details soon enough. Leave that to me."

"Very well. Do you need anything else?"

"Yes. Sean Wyatt's friend is in charge of the IAA."

"Tommy Schultz?"

"I think he may be of use to us. Find him. We'll use him as leverage."

14

MIAMI

Sean and Giulia stood on the sidewalk across the street from the unassuming bookstore. They opened earlier than most of the businesses in the area—but to be fair, those were mostly composed of bars and nightclubs.

The Hidden Gem bookshop was one of only a handful of retail businesses on the street, along with a coffee shop, a Cuban bakery, and a breakfast joint with a line out the door half a block long.

Arriving late the previous evening, Sean went through the processes he'd discussed on the plane—the rental cars, the hotel rooms, the whole nine.

He always kept two additional passports on his person at almost all times, particularly when on a job such as this.

The forged documents allowed him to pass through customs with total anonymity, and enabled him to do numerous other things under assumed names.

Security had changed over the years. Now airports use facial recognition software, even retinal scans at some of the more capable locations. Big Brother was getting more and more invasive as the years went by and as the technological capabilities rapidly evolved.

"I wonder why they open so early," Giulia said, staring at the bookshop with measured apprehension.

The two had waited on the sidewalk under a palm tree planted in a soil square amid the concrete. The street was lined with the tall plants. The broad leaves rustled in the morning sea breeze, waving back and forth in a subtle dance.

The sun hadn't appeared yet over the tops of the buildings, but if they'd been at South Beach only a half mile away, they'd have seen it well on its way into the cloudless Miami sky.

Cars passed by carrying people to their jobs along with maybe a dozen upright scooters, favored by the young and hip and pressed for time in Miami. Pedestrians passed, too, most of them stopping to get a bite to eat or a cup of coffee before heading to work. No one seemed to be paying any attention to Sean and Giulia.

That was the point of their standing on the sidewalk—to observe.

Even with all the caution Sean had exercised, all the steps he'd taken to ensure their safety, there was still a chance that none of it had worked. And it was safer to operate under the assumption that the henchmen from the Rossi Clan knew they were in Miami, and were aware of their next destination—the Hidden Gem bookshop.

A two-door Bentley drove by with the speaker system turned up to what had to be a deafening level for the occupant. What assaulted Sean's senses more was the color the owner had chosen to paint the expensive vehicle—flamingo pink.

He cringed as the car passed and stopped at the next light eighty feet away.

"Why do Americans like to listen to their music so loud?" Giulia asked. A similar disgusted look painted her face.

"Only a few do," Sean said. "Usually those with self-esteem issues. It's often a cry for attention. Like painting a work of art that color."

She snickered at his comment, but he wasn't kidding. Sean had studied psychology in college and had maintained an interest in the subject, and in human behavior, ever since. While he loved history and all things surrounding that subject, psychology had proved useful for him on many levels during his time with Axis, and with the

IAA. The things he'd learned in the psych program, along with his natural ability to read body language and understand people's motives, were a potent asset in the field.

"What color is your car?" Giulia asked, suddenly curious about the subject.

"Black. All my cars are black. Most of my motorcycles are, too, with a few exceptions."

"You ride motorcycles?" She sounded surprised.

He smirked. "Not as much as I'd like."

"What does your wife say about that?"

Sean turned his head and leveled his gaze. He didn't flinch, didn't crack. "She would say she's faster than me."

He looked back to the bookshop, then down the sidewalk to the left. He hadn't noticed anything suspicious or unusual, and they'd been standing in this spot for ten minutes. If someone were going to pop out and try to make a move on them, they'd have done it by now. Unless, of course, they were waiting patiently like a fisherman on a pond.

If the Rossi Clan had been able to track their location, any of their henchmen might simply be sitting by until they entered the bookstore. Once inside, they'd be cornered. Or their plan may have been to wait until Sean and Giulia left the shop with whatever item they'd uncovered while inside.

There were a couple of ways they could be ambushed, but doing it in the bookshop made the most sense. Out here on the street there were too many witnesses on their morning commute. It would be anarchy if a death squad started lighting the place up with gunfire—even if that sort of thing did happen in certain parts of Miami with alarming regularity.

"Should we go in?" Giulia asked. "Or are we just going to stand out here like a couple of tourists waiting for a bus with no stop?"

Sean chuckled. She had moxie. He had to give her that. She'd felt all prim and proper when he first met her—a first impression of someone who is all business and no play. Maybe he'd been wrong about that.

"Let's go," he said.

They waited for the light to change then crossed the street to the entrance of the bookshop.

A metal sign colored in light green with dark green lettering displaying the name hung out over the entrance—a recessed, black wooden door. A yellow butterfly was imprinted on a book next to the shop's name.

"Interesting choice of logo," Sean said, noting that both the building and the sign appeared to be quite old. The sign looked to have been repainted, probably many times over the decades.

"That can't be a coincidence," Giulia said.

Sean felt the locket in his pocket to make sure it was still there. His fingers pressed against the object before he reached out and opened the door, holding it for Giulia to enter. As she passed, he surveyed the street in both directions, paying particular attention to a row of shrubs just down from where he'd been standing. The bushes grew next to the curb. They were dark and dense, but if someone were behind them, he'd have noticed before from where they were standing. And even if a tail had rushed over and hid behind them, Sean would see their feet from here.

He wasn't exactly comfortable with this setup, but it was good enough for now. Sean would have preferred not to be boxed in. He knew the front door wasn't the only exit but hadn't had time to evaluate the shop to get a handle on the layout.

The door closed behind him as he followed Giulia inside. The smell of books and coffee enveloped him. He loved that scent. It always took him back to his college days when he would visit the university library. Of course, in those days, he wasn't surrounded by a combination of new and old books. They were mostly aged copies, unlike in mainstream retail bookstores, where the latest bestsellers lined shelves along every inch of available space.

This shop was a mix of both, an intoxicating paper-infused blend of the old and the new, and of course the java brewing at a counter in the rear of the cavernous room.

Directly in front of them, a round table filled with the latest thrillers stood in the middle of the floor. Another similar to it was a few steps beyond. To the right, a wide bookshelf brimmed with eight rows of the volumes. A sign over the top proclaimed them to be *USA Today* Bestsellers.

Sean frowned at the sign but ignored the question bubbling in his brain.

"Hello," a woman said from behind a checkout counter to the left. "Is there anything I can help you find?"

Sean and Giulia faced the direction where the voice came from.

The woman wore a dark green shirt and a black apron over it. Based on the accent and her appearance, Sean surmised she was of Cuban descent. Her dark brown hair hung in curls down to her neck, framing her face like a painting.

Sean smiled back at her as he approached the counter with Giulia close behind him.

"We have sort of a strange question, actually," Sean said, trying not to sound uncomfortable.

The young woman didn't seem fazed. Maybe it was too early. But she definitely looked curious.

"That sounds interesting. I love a strange question."

"You wouldn't happen to be the owner of this place, would you?"

The question puzzled her for a moment before she shook her head. "That's not a strange question. But no, I'm not the owner. I manage the place for the owners. They're rarely in here. I can give them a message if you like. But they won't be back for several days. They're out of town at the moment."

Sean felt a sinking sensation from his chest to his gut, like a rock dropping into a mud puddle.

"Oh." It was rare for Sean to find himself at a loss for words, but this was one of those moments. He hadn't even considered the possibility that Yolanda's grandchildren might not be around. In hindsight, it was a foolish assumption.

"We were hoping," Giulia said, stepping into the conversation, "to ask them a few questions."

"About books? If you're looking for something rare, we do have a selection of first editions in the walk-in display in the back." She pointed to the rear-left corner of the room, where a room made of cedar and glass protruded from the wall.

Even from fifty feet away, Sean saw that the books contained within the little room were much older than the rest of the stock put out on display.

"That's very cool," Sean said, staring at the room.

"Yes, I think so, too," the manager said. "It was a walk-in humidor thirty or so years ago. Before I was born."

The last little tidbit stung Sean's ego, reminding him of how old he was. He also wondered about using a humidor as a place to store books.

"We lowered the humidity," she said, sensing the question simmering on the top of his head. "Instead of between 70 to 72 percent humidity for cigars, we keep the room closer to 50, which is more of an optimal level for preservation of paper."

Sean nodded. "Impressive. Do we need a key to look in that room?"

"Yes. I have it right here if you'd like to take a look."

"Please. That would be great."

"Of course. No problem." The manager, whose name tag read Ahira, pulled out a drawer to her left, removed a single key attached to a ring shaped like a guitar pick. Sean tried to read the letters on the pick, but all he could see were G-I-D and part of a man's leg against a red background. The rest was covered with her thumb.

"Right this way," she said, flipping up a counter door and walking through it.

As Sean followed, he swept his gaze across the store, checking each row along the way, as well as taking a look back to the front to make sure no one had slipped in behind them. That would have been difficult with the bell that alerted the store manager whenever someone entered the shop.

A question from before reentered his mind as they continued toward the old humidor.

"I noticed you have a shelf for *USA Today* bestsellers. Why not the—"

"*New York Times*?" Ahira finished with an over-the-shoulder smile at him.

"Yeah."

"Because the *Times* is a curated list. *USA Today* is based on pure sales volume across multiple platforms. We prefer to let the readers decide what the best books are, and that paper is more in tune with that line of thought."

"Oh," he realized. "I never knew that."

"We have a selection of independent books here, too, stuff that has slipped past the mainstream eyeballs in the big publishing houses. I can recommend some if you're interested."

"Thanks," Sean said. "That would be great. I do a lot of traveling and could use a good book."

They reached the back of the store and the door into the humidor. Sean looked over at the barista—a guy who looked like he was twenty years old. He was engrossed by something on his phone and hadn't even noticed the group approaching the rare book collection.

"You don't happen to have anything about butterflies in this room, do you?" Giulia ventured.

Ahira inserted the key, turned it, and opened the door. She thought for a second before answering. "I'm not sure. Feel free to browse the inventory. If you would like me to take something out for you, I'm happy to help."

She held the door open for Sean and Giulia as they entered the room. The scent of cedar blended with old pages. Sean loved it immediately and wished he'd considered something similar in his study back in Atlanta. Such a room wouldn't be possible on the same scale since his library was barely larger than the antique humidor. That didn't keep him from wishing.

Giulia moved to the left and Sean to the right, each spying the titles and authors on the spines of the weathered tomes. Some of the books were in excellent condition, judging by nothing more than their exteriors. Others appeared to have been owned by either ravenous readers or multiple people who passed them down through time without much care to the condition.

Still, each one of these was valuable in its own way—all a precious representation of original work by authors who lived long ago.

The list of names on the books was impressive to say the least. Having spent a good amount of time studying fiction in school, Sean had a keen appreciation for great literature.

He paused at a collection of Edgar Poe's work and admired it. "Is that—"

"They're all real," Ahira answered, standing close behind the two visitors. "You want to have a closer look?"

He did, but Sean had to reel himself back on task. "Maybe some other time."

They continued looking across the spines.

Sean finished scanning the books on the top shelf, then proceeded down until he'd seen them all on the right half of the center shelf. He turned and continued the process on the left side while Giulia continued along the main bookshelf.

All the volumes contained in the room would make an excellent addition to any collection, but he wasn't here for that sort of thing. He needed to find something that would connect Isabella Fernandez's family to Yolanda Perez.

He crouched down low, tilting his head at an angle as he inspected the last row on the bottom of the bookshelf.

He'd nearly given up when he stopped at a book with an olive-green spine without a title or an author name. Only a faded image adorned the side of the book—a butterfly.

The book wasn't particularly big. In fact, as far as thickness was concerned, it would be considered a short read compared to all the other books in the room. And there was no clue as to what its pages might contain. Was it fiction? Nonfiction? Some kind of reference book?

Sean caught himself holding his breath. *No way it was going to be this easy. They walk in and go straight to the book? There had to be* more, and daring to hope for a simple solution almost always resulted in disappointment. He looked back up at the store manager. "This one," he said, pointing at the tome. "Could we please have a look at it?"

Giulia spun around and stared where he was pointing. Her eyes widened, as if in disbelief.

"Certainly," Ahira said.

She turned to a white wooden end table just inside the door and pulled open the only drawer. She pulled out a pair of white gloves from a stack within and slipped them onto her hands before moving past Sean and carefully removing the book from the shelf.

Ahira returned to the end table and laid the volume down on the surface. "If you would like to have a look yourself, please use the gloves provided in this drawer."

Sean nodded. "Thank you. I *would* like to."

He took out a pair of gloves and slid them onto his fingers. She didn't seem bothered by how quickly he answered.

Sean peeled back the cover, revealing the first page.

It was signed, along with a hand-penned dedication.

"For Yolanda. You are a fountain of beauty."

The flourished name on the signature was a familiar one, a name Sean had just learned in Argentina.

Clarence Gibbs.

15

Giulia leaned over Sean's shoulder and read the entry. "Gibbs." She turned her head and looked at Sean. He did the same as the epiphany hit.

Sean shook his head. "Gibbs gave Yolanda this book. But why?" He looked up at Ahira. "You don't know anything about this book?"

The manager thought for a couple of seconds before shaking her head. "Sorry, I don't. Actually, I've never seen it before." She looked back to the front of the building. There was still no one there, but from the look on her face, Sean could tell she felt like she needed to get back to the register.

He'd also noticed the security cameras in every corner of the humidor.

"How much for this one?" Sean asked.

Ahira moved past him and crouched down to the spot on the shelf where the book had been positioned on the shelf. All the other places had a bar code sticker just in front of the spine on the wooden surface. But the spot where the Gibbs book had been had none.

"That's odd," she said. "No bar code."

"What?" Giulia asked.

The manager stood. "We stick bar codes on the shelves in front of the books so we can maintain the integrity of the covers. We try to keep all of these in as good a condition as possible. It seems this one doesn't have a bar code. I could look it up if you like."

Sean nodded. "That would be great if it isn't too much trouble."

"Of course. No trouble at all." She stepped close to Sean and gently turned the page to the one with the title. "*The Life and Designs of Richard Morris Hunt*," she said, reading the text out loud. "I wonder why that one would be in here."

"What do you mean?" Giulia asked.

"Well, all the books in here are fiction or poetry. Seems an unusual match. That's all."

"Indeed," Sean said.

"I'll go check the inventory on the computer and see what we're selling it for. You'll be okay here while I go do that?"

"Yes. If it's okay for us to stay here and look through this."

"Of course. I'll be back in a moment."

She left the little room and closed the door behind her.

"What do you think it means?" Giulia wondered.

Sean studied the title page for ten seconds and then turned to the next. The first picture on the following page was of a granite monument. The curved structure featured a bronze bust of a man with a mustache and clothing that would have been typical for the late nineteenth century. Two steps led up to the figure, which was set back in the design of the monument to focus the attention of a visitor. Pillars wrapped around him, supporting granite slabs. On one end of the U-shaped structure, a statue stood holding a paint pallet. Opposite, another figure held something else, but Sean couldn't make out exactly what.

Underneath the image, the text read, Richard Morris Hunt Memorial.

"Who was this person?" Giulia whispered. "I have never heard of him."

Sean admitted he didn't know. "This is a new name for me, too."

He took out his phone and entered the query. The answer came back almost instantly.

He read the text on the screen and summarized it. "This says he was one of the most prestigious architects during the Gilded Age. Apparently, he did a lot of designs for many wealthy and influential people of the time."

Giulia didn't see the connection. "Why would Gibbs leave this book here with Perez?"

"I'm not sure," Sean confessed. "But it's a miracle the thing is still here. Bookstores go through so much inventory, it's a wonder this one didn't end up being sold, or simply being donated to a library or to a museum."

He glanced through the glass as Ahira walked through the counter opening and stopped behind the computer at the register.

"True. But that doesn't tell us what we're supposed to do next."

"I think it does," Sean countered. "This image of the Hunt monument. What if the monument is where we'll find the diamond?"

"Do you really think so?" Giulia said, hope tickling her voice.

Sean shrugged. "It's hard to say." He leaned closer and inspected the image further, then turned the page to see if there was anything else that might lend a clue. The first chapter talked about the life of the architect, how it began in Brattleboro, Vermont.

He turned back to the image of the monument. Something about it drew him in. But he wasn't sure.

Is this where the diamond was hidden? In the middle of Manhattan, in plain sight?

"What are you thinking?" Giulia asked.

Sean didn't answer right away. He turned the page again and kept going until he found another picture.

"Oh wow," he breathed.

"What?" Giulia stared at the image of a spectacular palace. The black-and-white aerial photo displayed a massive structure surrounded by forests and hills.

He passed her a sidelong glance. "You don't know what that is?"

She shook her head, and her expression conveyed the same ignorance. "Looks like a palace somewhere in Europe."

She wasn't wrong. It did portray that appearance, which was no accident on the part of the designer.

"That's in the mountains of North Carolina," Sean said.

"Here? In America?"

"Yes."

"I didn't know you had such palaces here."

"We don't. Not in the traditional sense. I guess that would technically be called a mansion, but to the level of opulence of some of the greatest palaces in Europe. That is the Biltmore Estate."

She blinked for a moment, thinking. Then her eyes lit up. "Oh, yes. Of course. I have heard of this place."

"It's a famous estate, for sure. Commodore Vanderbilt was one of the wealthiest men in the world during the Gilded Age. He owned a vast majority of the railroads in this country. If you wanted to move anything by rail, he got a cut. His wealth was rivaled only by a handful of others—Carnegie, Morgan, Rockefeller.

"His descendants were patrons of the arts and culture. I can't recall exactly, but I believe his daughter ended up moving to Europe because of all that." Sean's eyes fell to the picture again. "I didn't know who the architect was until now."

He continued turning the pages, careful not to tear the edges of the delicate paper. "Wow," Sean exclaimed quietly. "Scroll and Key. That's the secret society house for Skull and Bones at Yale." On the next page, he noted another building at Yale University that Hunt had designed. "This guy was the hottest architect of his day."

Sean caught movement near the front of the store. The door opened. He and Giulia barely heard the bell ding from inside the humidor.

Two men walked in wearing light windbreakers and jeans. Sunglasses concealed their eyes. Both of them had the same look as the men he'd killed in Argentina.

"Get down," Sean said.

Before Giulia could protest, he put his hand on her head and gently pushed her toward the floor. He lowered himself at the same time, dipping below the wooden wall that held up the huge panes of glass surrounding the room.

"What is it?" she hissed.

"Trouble."

16

The first stop Sean had made when they arrived back in the States was at a friend's place in Homestead near Miami—a friend with a federal firearm license who used to operate his own gun shop out of his garage.

This wasn't just any garage. The reinforced concrete block structure sat off to the right of Terry's four-thousand-square-foot home. It was one of those places people hang vintage gas station signs on the exterior walls. The inside, however, wasn't anything like a car garage.

Beyond the doors, Terry's shop was a firearm aficionado's paradise, filled with racks and glass cases of nearly every type of legal gun one could imagine.

Terry had been more than accommodating for his out-of-state friend. While Sean couldn't purchase a firearm since he was from another state, Terry *could* give him some weapons and simply transfer the paperwork associated with the serial number on the lower receivers. Sean knew the State of Florida considered guns to be private property, and as such can be transferred to another person with little to no hassle.

Giulia had also been taken aback by how easily and quickly Sean could get a firearm on such short notice—two firearms, to be exact. A pair of Springfield XD 9mm subcompact single stacks.

She'd balked at the notion of using a gun for anything, but he figured she would either get on board with it or he'd simply have two weapons. He would have preferred to carry his usual .40-caliber XD with a full-capacity magazine, but the single stack was more easily concealed, though he didn't like the narrow feel of the weapon in his hands. Still, discretion was king. No sense in worrying others with the sight of a pistol grip sticking up out of his belt.

He had a conceal-carry holster for such weapons back home, but they felt bulky and uncomfortable tucked inside the waist of his pants. These slim models were much easier to deal with, and packed enough stopping power for someone as lethal as Sean.

Giulia's attitude about the guns didn't surprise him. Sean knew several Europeans who acted the same way about firearms. One of his close friends didn't understand what he called "American gun culture" and the love affair with the weapons.

Sean had long ago given up the notion of trying to explain it, always leaving it with the same comment. "If bad guys have guns, I'll have them, too. No sense in giving evil an advantage."

When he put it that way, she seemed to accept it, albeit with significant reluctance.

Still, he carried both weapons with him to make her a little more comfortable with the situation.

Now, he wondered if she was glad they'd made the purchase.

"Looks like we were followed," Sean whispered. He peeked up over the edge of the wooden paneling and saw the two men walk up to the counter where Ahira stood. Fear snaked through Sean's gut.

They'd unintentionally put the manager in danger, as well as the barista in the back. He glanced over at the guy still standing by the espresso machine, staring at his phone.

Whatever he was doing must have been truly engrossing—probably checking out Instagram models or scrolling through YouTube Shorts.

Sean drew the pistol from his side, held it up near his shoulder, and chambered a round.

"Remember what I taught you?"

Fear smacked Giulia across the face with the realization of what he was asking her to do. She shook her head vehemently. "No. I can't."

"You sure?" he asked. Deep down, he knew that would be her reaction. It didn't surprise him. Not in the least.

"Definitely."

He'd given her a few pointers in the car, showed her how to handle the weapon, how to squeeze the trigger instead of pulling it, how to point and shoot without thinking too much about what she was seeing or feeling.

"Okay," Sean said, turning his attention back to the men at the front. They were talking to Ahira.

To her credit, she seemed to either be completely composed, or entirely aloof to the danger. Sean figured it had to be the latter.

It was a warm morning, as most were in Miami. And these two guys had jackets on. The only possible reason for that would be they were hiding guns. But Sean had a bad feeling that would change the second they saw him and Giulia.

"We need to get out the back," Sean whispered.

"How?"

"There was an exit sign behind the coffee counter over a door. That must lead behind the building, maybe to an alley or something."

"They'll see us if we try to get out that way,' she protested.

"Not if we're quiet."

Sean wasn't going to keep the debate going. If they stayed here, they were cornered, with only two extra magazines and very little cover. On top of it, they were surrounded by glass, which would only complicate things. He remembered watching the greatest Christmas movie of all time in the 1980s where the fabled cop John McClane cut up his feet walking around barefoot on broken glass.

Of course, Sean had no intention of removing his shoes, but there were plenty of other ways glass shards could cause problems, particularly if they were exploding in toward his and Giulia's faces.

He reached up and grasped the doorknob.

"Sean," Giulia hissed.

He froze and looked at her. He'd thought the discussion about the plan was over.

"The book," she said, indicating the tome with a nod.

"Right." He reached over and closed the book, remaining low as he did so. Then he turned and handed it to Giulia. "You're going to have to carry it while I cover us. You see the coffee counter?"

She said that she did.

"Follow me past that last row of books. Once we're behind that, we have good cover until we reach the center aisle. From there, we'll keep going behind the next row, then up the stairs to the coffee bar."

"What about the barista?" Giulia asked. Her eyes flashed to the guy standing by the espresso machine, still staring with glazed eyes at his phone.

"I'm still working on that."

He reached up again and turned the doorknob. Thankfully, it didn't make a sound as the latch retreated from the housing in the frame.

When they'd entered the old humidor, the door's hinges hadn't creaked either, but now Sean doubted himself, questioning whether or not he'd even paid attention to that minute detail—one that was quickly swelling into a potential cataclysm.

He held his breath as he pushed the door open. It didn't make a sound.

No sense of relief filled him, though. This was merely the first step. He looked over at Giulia and held his finger to his lips to signal silence—probably redundant at this point—then leaned out through the opening.

If the men at the front counter had seen the door open, there'd be trouble. But as Sean stole a quick look their way, he saw that both men were intently focused on Ahira.

The last thing he wanted was for bullets to start flying and for her to be hit by one that went astray.

Satisfied for the moment, Sean led the way on hands and knees, crawling out through the door and around the corner of the last row of books. Once there, he stopped and looked back, holding up the gun in front of him to both be ready to return fire and to keep the weapon concealed from the aloof barista.

"There were two of them. Where are they?" Sean heard one of the men at the front ask.

To her credit, Ahira must have sensed the danger and been deflecting the men's questions.

Giulia reached the back row and crouched behind Sean as he watched around the corner.

Sean stood up and peeked over the shoulder-high shelf at the two men.

"What are you? Cops?" Ahira asked.

Sean nearly chuckled at the question, but this was no time to laugh. No matter how much he appreciated her moxie.

"Yes," one of them lied.

Sean ducked back down out of sight and took out his phone.

"What are you doing?" Giulia asked, her voice barely above a breath.

"Backup plan," he said. "In case we don't get out of here."

Fear swept through her eyes. Her chin dropped, and her mouth gaped. "What?"

Sean sent a quick text message and then shoved the phone back in his pocket.

"Always good to have a backup plan," Sean whispered. "Come on."

He led the way to the end of the row and then peeked around the corner, still keeping the gun shielded from the barista in case the guy ever took his eyes off the phone in his hands.

Sean saw the two men still standing there at the counter.

"I'm going to need to see some kind of ID if you're cops," Ahira pressed. "You got badges or something?"

Sean grinned at the response. He was about to turn and head toward the steps when another voice broke the relative silence.

"Can I help you two with something?"

The grin on Sean's face vaporized.

The jig was up. And he knew exactly what was going to happen next.

17

Tommy stepped out of the hotel room and walked down the corridor, pulling his suitcase behind him.

He turned into the alcove where the two elevator doors awaited and pressed the down arrow before stepping back to wait on the lift. While he stood there, he pulled on the right strap of his black backpack to tighten it.

It had been a good couple of days at the exhibit. But he was exhausted, and even the seven hours of sleep he'd gotten over the course of the night didn't seem like enough.

He rubbed his eyes as the elevator dinged to let him know it had arrived. Then the metallic doors opened, he stepped on, and hit the button for the lobby.

Tommy usually enjoyed travel. He often joked that he spent more time doing that than being at his home in the Virginia Highlands of Atlanta. But that was the nature of his job. Travel was an intricate part of it, and it always would be until he decided to retire... if he ever decided to retire.

For the time being, at least in his mind, that day was far off in a distant and unknowable future.

The lift descended quickly to the bottom of the hotel and stopped at the lobby. He stepped out onto the shiny black floor and made his way around the corner toward the exit.

His Uber driver would be here in three minutes—or so the app suggested. Most of the time he'd been happy with the service, with the few exceptions being when a driver abruptly dropped the ride. No explanation was ever given, and that could be frustrating—especially if someone were in a hurry.

He strolled by the concierge desk, smiling at the young woman behind the counter. She returned the gesture and with a bright white smile bade him a good day.

At the exit, the sliding doors parted in front of him, and he continued through, allowing the second set of doors to do the same.

Warm, humid air embraced him as he stepped outside and made his way past the valet podium, veering left to a spot where two other hotel patrons appeared to be waiting for rides.

Tommy let go of his suitcase and looked down at his phone, checking to make sure the driver was still on his way.

Ranu was only a minute away now, driving a black Toyota Camry.

Tommy had ridden in more Ubers than he could recall, but one detail he did remember was that most of them seemed to be Toyotas. And very often a Camry.

A black Chevy Suburban pulled up to the entrance underneath the awning and stopped in front of a couple who were dressed in expensive-looking clothes. Tommy smelled their cologne and perfume from ten feet away and twitched his nose.

He'd met those types many times. They had money. Nothing wrong with that. But he got the distinct impression with these two, as with many others, that they wanted people to know they had money.

Tommy's net worth had skyrocketed over the years. But he kept things pretty simple. He currently wore a gray Atlanta Braves T-shirt and jeans and some navy-blue OluKai boat shoes.

Sure, he had a spritz of Geir Ness at the base of his neck but only one pump.

He watched the couple load their luggage with the assistance of the driver and then climb in the back of the SUV. A minute later, the vehicle drove away, leaving Tommy alone in front of the hotel.

The app on his phone showed him that Ranu's car was just around the corner at the stoplight. Tommy didn't get his hopes up. There'd been a couple of occasions where the map displayed his ride close by and then abruptly shifted it several blocks away. He wondered if the GPS connected to the rideshare apps had a bug in it, but that was something the developers could have fixed long ago.

The car on the screen began moving again, and Tommy looked up to see the Camry come into view.

The windows were tinted so dark it was nearly impossible to see through them, and as a result the darkened interior only revealed a dim glimpse at the driver.

"No way those are below the legal window tint limit," Tommy muttered.

The law only allowed for windows to be smoked to a certain level. Beyond that, fines could be imposed on drivers whose glass was too dark. It was a reasonable law on multiple fronts. Drivers needed to be able to see out their windows at night, and if they were too dark, that became a safety issue. Furthermore, cops needed to be able to see inside a vehicle if they pulled someone over. Their jobs were hard enough.

Tommy often wondered if police ever got used to the tense moment of approaching a total stranger in a vehicle with no way of knowing what the person might be thinking.

The sedan's driver looped into the hotel entrance and stopped in front of Tommy. The passenger-side window rolled down a little. "Are you Tommy?" Ranu asked.

He was a clean-cut guy, late twenties, and wore a dark blue polo. He looked Italian, but with a name like Ranu he could have easily been of Middle Eastern origin, or perhaps even North African in certain spots.

"Yes, sir," Tommy said.

The man got out of the car and walked around to the trunk. "I'll help you with that," Ranu said with a pleasant smile. He was an inch shorter than Tommy and had an athletic figure like a guy who played soccer. His black hair was short, businesslike, which went with the aviator sunglasses that blocked his eyes from view.

"Thanks." Tommy took his hand off the suitcase handle as the trunk opened.

Ranu lifted the luggage into the trunk and then hit the button to send the lid back down again.

Tommy opened the back door to the car and climbed in, setting his backpack on the leather seat next to him, then closed the door and strapped on the seatbelt.

Ranu returned to the driver's seat, shifted the vehicle into drive, and pulled out of the hotel entryway.

"Going to the airport?" Ranu asked as he turned right onto the street.

It was the usual kind of confirmation question Tommy had come to expect from drivers even though they already knew where they were taking their fare.

"Yes."

Tommy expected another question, one that would spark up a forced conversation, but instead Ranu remained quiet. He had some soft music playing on the radio with a steady beat and subtle melody that reminded Tommy of traditional Japanese songs blended with modern electronic drums.

The phone in Tommy's pocket vibrated. He was about to take it out anyway to kill time on the way to the airport, so he pulled device from his pocket and checked the screen.

The preview was from Sean.

Tommy tapped on the message, and the text messaging app opened.

He read the message quietly, concern darkening his face with every word. "Richard Morris Hunt memorial in Manhattan. Don't respond. We've been followed."

There was nothing else. And Tommy knew there wouldn't be.

He didn't know why Sean would mention the location in New York City, though he could guess. Sean probably wanted his friend to meet him there, but the fact he said not to respond, and that they'd been followed, was troublesome.

Tommy looked up and through the windshield at the cars ahead of them on the road. Sean was in trouble. He wouldn't say it. That wasn't Sean's style.

Including the part about being followed suggested that Tommy use caution. He quickly deduced that meant Sean was heading to Manhattan one way or the other, either on his own or as a hostage. Tommy hoped it wasn't the latter.

Either way, Tommy was going to have to change his travel plans. He was going to fly back to Atlanta within the next two hours, but now it seemed his destination was New York.

The driver abruptly turned off the street and into a parking area behind an old seafood restaurant that looked as if it hadn't been open for business in five years. Plywood covered the windows. Graffiti adorned the walls over the faded and peeling original paint. The asphalt, too, was crumbling in several places, and Tommy felt the bumps as the car rolled over the cracks and holes.

"Sorry," Ranu said before Tommy could ask what he was doing. "I missed my turn."

He spun the wheel as if to turn around but instead guided the vehicle behind the dilapidated building. Then he hit the gas pedal and accelerated forward so fast that Tommy felt himself pushed against his seat.

Ranu twisted the wheel to the left and slammed on the brakes behind the building—out of sight from the main drag, and any other cars or people who might pass by.

Tommy saw two other vehicles parked just ahead of them—a pair of black Cadillac Escalades. Four men stood outside the vehicles, each with hands folded in front of them. They wore windbreakers over T-shirts, and Tommy knew exactly why. They were armed.

Before he could react, Ranu turned and pointed a pistol at Tommy's face, the long suppressor barrel only inches from his nose.

"Get out."

Tommy steeled his nerves, inhaling calmly through his nose. "So, we're not going to the airport?"

"Now."

"Fine. But I'm leaving a one-star review." It occurred to Tommy that this was probably not the real Ranu, and he immediately wondered where the poor Uber driver was if that were the case.

Two of the men by the SUVs moved toward the car, stepping around the passenger's side to the back door where Tommy sat.

One with a shaved head pulled the door open, while the other brandished a pistol. "Get out."

"Do you guys always repeat each other's commands?"

The one standing outside the door with the pistol reached in and grabbed Tommy's collar. He jerked him out with surprising strength, which was no easy feat considering Tommy's muscular physique.

He spun him around and shoved him at the other guy, who caught him with both hands and twisted around so Tommy faced away from him.

Tommy felt the muzzle of a suppressor dig into his back. It was a dull pain, one that would probably leave a bruise. He'd felt it before. And each time he found himself in a situation like this, he questioned his life decisions for the last few decades.

"Take it easy," Tommy complained. The order produced a deeper shove of the silencer into his back. He winced and stumbled forward. "What do you guys want?"

None of them answered.

The thug with his gun in Tommy's back shoved him into the front of the SUV on the right. Tommy caught himself, slapping his palms against the hood.

He turned around in time for another goon to shove him into the grill again. "Hands up high," the guy ordered.

Tommy complied. The man patted him down, then reached into his front pocket.

"Hey. You have to at least buy me dinner first."

The goon ignored him and removed the phone from his pocket.

He tapped the screen, which displayed the facial ID unlock option. He turned it around and pointed it at Tommy's face.

Tommy looked away, unwilling to look at the device to allow these guys access. But another of the gunmen stepped up, grabbed his head with both hands, and forced him to face the screen.

Resistance was futile. The phone unlocked as it recognized Tommy's face.

The guy with the phone checked the text messages and saw the last one the phone had received.

A dark, satisfied grin crossed his face. "Put him in the back."

Two of the men grabbed Tommy on either side and ushered him back to the rear of the vehicle.

He dragged his feet, resisting every step of the way. Despite being stronger than either of the men abducting him, their combined strength was too much. Not that it mattered. Where would he go? Even if he could have fought them off, they and the others were armed. They'd just kill him and leave him there. Or worse, shoot him in the foot or kneecap to immobilize him and squash his pitiful resistance.

The guy on his right forced Tommy's arm behind his back. Then the left arm. The other wrapped a zip tie around his wrists and clicked it until the plastic dug into his skin.

Once his hands were secured, they shoved him into the cargo area of the SUV and closed the door.

At the front of the vehicle, the man with Tommy's phone took out his own device, found the last number in the call list, and hit the green button.

He held the phone to his ear while it rang.

"Do you have him?" a gruff voice asked through the speaker.

"Yes. We have him. And we know where Wyatt is going, too."

18

All the barista had to do was keep his eyes on his phone and his big mouth shut. It was so simple. The guy had barely moved since Sean and Giulia entered the building, and had seemingly paid no attention while Ahira showed them to the renovated humidor.

Now, of all times, he opened his yap.

Sean held an index finger to his mouth and shook his head. But it was too late. He saw the barista's expression turn from curious to terrified. And Sean knew why.

He imagined the men at the front counter had drawn their firearms, with at least one of them making a move toward the rear of the building—probably down the center aisle.

"You, get down there," one of the thugs barked. "If you get up, you die."

He must have been talking to Ahir because the barista didn't move, and the voice hadn't been directed that way.

The barista took a step backward, fear widening his eyelids.

Sean had two options. Sit there and wait for the gunmen to show themselves or go on the offensive.

"Get down," Sean mouthed at the frightened barista. The guy

didn't see him. He was too focused on something or someone at the front of the store.

Sean knew he'd get down the second bullets started flying.

If the assailants were smart, they would split up and go down the outer aisles along the wall, then work their way in. Once they found Sean and Giulia, the crossfire would easily take them down.

Sean couldn't let that happen.

Gripping his pistol so the barista could see it, he turned and mouthed "Stay here" to Giulia, then crept back to the other end of the bookshelf, stopping at the corner across from the humidor.

He listened closely, glancing back at Giulia, who'd remained frozen on the floor.

Something rustled from around the corner. It was difficult to estimate how far away, but Sean guessed twenty feet. He didn't know what made the sound—a gunman's pants swishing together, a book poster flapping as he walked by, or had it just been Sean's imagination?

Sean had to shoot first. That much he knew. But spinning around the corner and locking the sights on the target was another thing.

He clenched his teeth, steadied his breathing, and twisted around the bookshelf with the 9mm extended out.

The gunman was halfway down the aisle to Sean's position, and had been in the middle of checking a row when Sean appeared.

The man tried to turn and protect himself, whipping a pistol to the right, but his reaction wasn't fast enough. Sean fired two shots, one in the gut and one into the upper chest.

The guy fell backward onto the floor like a sack of sand.

Smoke filled Sean's nostrils with the all-too-familiar smell of spent powder. The other gunman would have been equally caught off guard by the gunfire. If he and the other man were working in tandem, keeping the same pace as they searched each row, it was likely the second assassin would have not only heard what happened but seen it as well.

Sean hurried back over to Giulia and handed her the second pistol. She shook her head, but he wouldn't take no for an answer.

She reluctantly accepted the weapon, probably now because the gunfire had forced the grim reality on her that they were in a very real gunfight. And the last thing anyone wanted to do in a gunfight is not have a gun—even if she had never used one before.

Sean hoped it didn't come down to that. Most people weren't emotionally equipped to handle killing. He never understood why he had been so immune to its usual effects, but that numbness also carried with it a more frightening burden.

He'd worked through that over the years, his strange sense of purpose in taking out the world's evil trash. But doing so had also caused more questions to bubble to the murky surface of his soul.

Sean quickly ducked around the corner and aimed down the center aisle. No sign of the other guy, which confirmed his suspicion that the man would be moving along the opposite wall from his partner.

The second Sean failed to see the second gunman, he darted across the aisle, careful to make as little noise as possible. He kept his head down and waited for a second. It was a game of cat and mouse now. The gunman could either approach down the row directly behind Sean's back, and step around the corner for a point-blank kill —or he could continue along the far wall and appear at the other end of the bookshelf.

Sean had moved up one row toward the front when he crossed to keep Giulia from being in the immediate line of fire. At least this way, Sean guaranteed he'd be the first one spotted.

He shifted his feet to keep his body in the main aisle while using the end of the bookshelf for cover, then leaned around to the right.

The man was standing at the other end with his pistol extended, as if he'd anticipated Sean's play.

The muzzle puffed.

Sean jumped back as the bullets cracked through air, narrowly missing his head.

He ducked low, reached the pistol around the bookshelf, and took two blind shots down the row.

He had no misgivings about hitting the target, though that little miracle would have been gratefully accepted. But those two shots were meant to drive the guy back and give Sean the chance to go on the offensive again.

What he didn't anticipate was what happened next.

The front door to the bookshop burst open, and two more gunmen stepped through.

"Oh, come on," Sean muttered as he pushed hard against the floor with every muscle his legs could offer. He took one step and dove into the opposite row just as the gunmen at the front opened fire.

Bullets snapped through the air behind him, again barely missing their mark. Some of the rounds sank into the wooden façade of the coffee bar. As the shooters adjusted their aim for the moving target, more rounds tore through books and sent scraps of paper and wood into the air in plumes.

It took a lot to make Sean uncomfortable, but these guys had done it.

There was no way he could have anticipated the reinforcements storming through the front. At least, that's what he told himself with a dose of bitter regret.

There was no time for such thoughts. His brainpower had to be focused on the here and now.

His elite training and years spent in the field with two agencies kicked in, and he surrendered to instincts forged in a fiery crucible.

He needed to flank the enemy, but doing so would leave Giulia out in the open where she was crouched behind the last row of books. His only option was to draw their fire and force them to focus solely on him.

The plan took less than two seconds to formulate in his mind before he stood up and opened fire over the top of the bookshelf.

Just like his blind shot around the corner before, this one had a similar effect. The rounds sailed high over the targets—an intentional move to avoid accidentally hitting the store manager, who was out of sight behind the counter.

Both the shooters ducked while the other across the room reemerged in the same row as Sean.

One of them fired again as Sean sprinted around the corner near the wall and rushed toward the front of the building.

Stopping at the end of another row, he ducked down, ejected the magazine to check it, then shoved it back into the well. He still had two full mags on him, but wasting rounds was never a good idea. Especially when outnumbered.

Sean remained in place for a moment, listening for any sign of movement from the other three men. If they were moving, they were doing so with extreme care. Even so, the subtlest sounds could give them away.

Sean heard the slightest squeak of a shoe to his left and raised his weapon as a gunman appeared around the corner of the row at the front of the room.

The pistol in Sean's hand spit twice, plowing two rounds through the man's chest—each within four inches of the other.

Ejecting the empty magazine from the weapon, Sean quickly replaced it, dropped the slide, and rushed toward his most recent victim.

The man coughed and gurgled. Blood splattered around his face and soaked his shirt.

Sean took the guy's pistol with the suppressor and put the guy out of his misery with a single shot through the head.

He knew the muted pop would flush out the others, and he wasn't wrong.

The second newcomer spun around the end of the bookshelf into the center aisle and fired as Sean rolled forward toward the checkout counter. The bullets shredded through book covers on the shelf lining the wall.

He steadied his balance as he crouched on one knee and kept his sights aimed down the row. He was exposed here and felt immediately uncomfortable. But he had one more trick up his sleeve.

Both men would be converging on his position now—or so he hoped. If that weren't the case, then the one who'd been on the opposite side of the room had located Giulia, and that would present its own set of problems.

No. They would go after the threat. And Sean was definitely a threat.

He leaned against the surface of the bookshelf's end and held both weapons up near his chest.

If these guys were smart, they'd each take a row on either side of the bookshelf, and flank Sean from both sides.

He steadied his breathing again and leaned into the shelf's end. If they did flank him, he'd have to take out both men on either side. Timing that would be difficult, and they would have the advantage of surprise, and likely a quicker draw.

The odds weren't good.

As he pushed against the end of the shelf, he felt the narrow end shelves that contained more books—in this case, a selection of science fiction stories.

Sean enjoyed reading sci-fi when he was traveling. That and fantasy were two of his favorite genres.

Not that fiction could help him right now. Or could it?

A crazy idea popped into his head. It was a long shot, but given the circumstances, worth the risk.

He turned around, grabbed a book with a silver spaceship sitting in a barn on the cover, and flung it high over the top of the shelf.

The pages flapped in the air as it flew toward the center aisle. Sean spun around to his left and into the row, locking in on his target with the 9mm in his right hand, and fired.

The assassin was halfway to Sean's position, but the flying book had distracted him just enough. His head was tilted up at an angle; the pistol in his hand dipped slightly so the muzzle was pointed at the floor to the right of Sean's feet.

The round caught the man in the chest and knocked him back a step. As he stumbled, Sean finished the job with another round to the head and rushed forward, passing the guy as he fell to the ground.

Now there was only one left.

Sean snuck to the other end and listened.

The last man standing could have been mere feet away just on the other side of the row. If he were on the move, Sean couldn't hear him.

Edging around the end of the shelf and into the center aisle, Sean aimed both pistols ahead of him. No sign of the gunman.

At the rear of the room, the coffee bar was also empty. He figured the barista had either run out the back or ducked down behind the counter. There was no sign of Giulia. Sean could only hope she was still okay, preferably hiding somewhere the bullets weren't flying.

Sean rounded the corner, both pistols still extended, but the gunman wasn't there.

Movement to Sean's right from behind the next row sent a chill through Sean's spine. He'd been caught assuming the other gunman would be in this row, not the next one over. And now, he'd been flanked.

He didn't even have time to turn his weapons at the killer.

"Drop them," the man said, his accent heavy Italian.

Sean took a deep breath, still unmoving. *Why hadn't the guy just killed him right then and there?*

The only explanation could be that whoever these guys worked for wanted Sean and Giulia, or at least one of them, alive.

"I said drop them. Don't make me ask again, or it will hurt."

Sean calculated the odds of getting out of this alive if he obeyed the man's orders. His brain also ran the numbers of likely outcomes were he to try something crazy. Dropping to the floor, rolling away while shooting came to mind. But that wasn't going to work. The assailant had the drop on him, and the slightest sudden movement would get Sean a bullet through the head.

"Do it slowly," the guy said. "Very slowly." His voice was calm but filled with what Sean could only describe as a dark purpose.

"Okay," Sean surrendered. "I'm putting them—"

A gunshot popped loudly and echoed around the room. For a second, Sean thought the gunman had shot him, but no pain accompanied the sound, and the noise had come from somewhere else.

He turned his head and saw the man grimacing, twisting his body around and changing his aim, pointing it down the row.

Sean snapped his hands around and fired with both weapons, each sending a round through the side of the guy's head.

He dropped to the floor, the pistol in his hand falling limp from his fingers.

"Giulia?" Sean said. "You okay?"

He passed the dead man and paused at the end of the bookshelf. "I'm coming around the corner. Don't shoot."

He stepped around the shelf and saw her standing fifteen feet away with the pistol gripped tightly in her hands, still held out at full extension.

"It's okay," he said. "I think we're good."

She slowly lowered the weapon. Her lips quivered, and her eyes were wide with disbelief. He knew why. She'd just shot someone for the first time.

Sean made his way over to her and took the pistol from her. "You didn't kill him," he said. "I did. But you saved my life."

She could only stare at the body sprawled out on the carpet. Her hands trembled.

"You did great," he added.

"I... shot him."

"Yes. Yes, you did. And if you hadn't, he might have killed us both." He looked to the front of the store and the vacant checkout counter. "I need to make sure Ahira is okay. Are you going to be all right?"

She nodded but said nothing, still shell-shocked from the turn of events.

He left her standing there and hurried to the front of the building. Before checking on the manager, he locked the front doors in case there were others still waiting outside to barge in and finish what they started.

Sean stepped over to the counter, worried he might find a bloodied Ahira crouching down behind the register.

Relief spilled over him when he saw her down on the floor, arms wrapped around her legs and her head down close to her knees.

"Ahira," Sean said in a soft tone.

Her head shot up, startled from the sound of her name. "It's you," she managed.

"It's okay. I need you to call the police. Can you do that for me?"

"Who were those guys?" she asked. "Why were they after you?"

"It's a long story."

To her credit, she seemed to be handling the situation better than expected. Some people would collapse in a heap, crying. Ahira stood up and surveyed the room as if it wasn't the first time she'd witnessed a violent shootout.

"You took all of them out?" she asked. There was no hiding the astonishment in her voice. "There were like four of them."

Sean nodded and blew it off. "I'm going to go in the back and make sure your barista is okay. I don't know what happened to him in the chaos."

"Hey, Chuy!" she shouted. It was Sean's turn to be startled. "You okay back there?"

Sean followed her gaze to the coffee bar in the back. Slowly, the top of the barista's black hair appeared, and then the rest of him as he stood up from behind the counter.

"I'm good," he said back, holding up a thumb.

Sean noticed the phone was still in the guy's other hand. "He's not going to post that online or something is he? I would rather not go viral if it's just the same to you."

Ahira shook her head. "Hey, if you're trying to post that somewhere, keep this guy out of it. Understand?"

"Sure. Okay," he said. His voice was unusually steady considering.

"You sure you're going to be all right?" Sean asked. "This is—"

"I've seen some stuff go down," she explained. "One of my cousins was in a gang."

Sean nodded. "I see. Well, I would hang back there behind the counter until the police arrive. I don't want you to have to see the carnage. I'm afraid your store is going to be closed for a while."

"It's okay. I needed the time off anyway."

Sean looked back toward the renovated humidor. "At least it looks like the most valuable collection wasn't damaged."

"No kidding." She stared at him for a long moment and then asked. "What did you say your name was, anyway?"

"I didn't."

Ahira inclined her head, studying him more closely, as if a stray hair or a freckle might give away his secret.

"One of those if-you-told-me-you'd-have-to-kill-me types?"

"No. Not anymore. My name is Sean Wyatt. The cops will probably want to know."

"You're not sticking around?"

"No. But they'll know how to find me if they need me."

She seemed to accept the answer, albeit with a suspicious glint in her eyes.

His phone started vibrating in his pocket, tearing him away from the conversation.

He took it out and looked at the number. It was Tommy.

"Hey, man," he said, holding the phone to his ear as he silently excused himself. "Right now isn't a great—"

"We have your friend."

The voice through the speaker wasn't Tommy. It was rough, like a dump truck filled with rocks.

"Who is this?"

"We also know where you're going. Manhattan? The Richard Morris Hunt Memorial?"

Sean's jaw tightened. His face heated with anger. "It's not polite to read other people's messages. The government doesn't like competition."

"Did you find what you were looking for in Miami?" the man asked, ignoring Sean's wisecrack.

"Maybe. I found four bodies here, too. You wouldn't happen to know them, would you?"

"Chelsea Pier," the man replied, ignoring the barb. "Our yacht is docked next to the driving range. And bring whatever you found in Miami."

"Which boat?" Sean growled.

"You needn't worry about that. When you arrive, we will take you aboard. If you try anything, your friend dies."

"If you—" The call ended before Sean could respond with a threat of his own.

His free hand tightened into an angry fist. But there was nothing he could do. For now.

Giulia appeared around the corner of the nearest bookshelf. "Who was that?"

Sean stared at the screen for several heartbeats. "I don't know. But they have Tommy."

19

Barone Totti fumed.

How could this have happened—not once, but twice?

By the time the cops were on the scene, he'd already driven away just as he had the first time Wyatt had taken out his men.

These guys weren't slouches. Each one of them was lethal, highly trained, and often brutal with their execution.

Sean Wyatt had taken out four of them as if he were swatting flies.

"You sure we shouldn't make sure all of them are—"

"They're dead," Totti spat to the guy in the driver's seat across from him. "Head to the airport."

He'd kept one of the men with him just in case—a tank of a man named Luciano. Now, he wasn't so sure he shouldn't have sent him in, too. Then again, if four couldn't get the job done, what would one more do?

In some situations, it was better to retreat and live to fight another day.

Luciano steered around the corner to the right and kept driving, heading toward downtown Miami.

"How could you know they're dead?"

"Because I know. The same thing happened before. Cops started showing up. Everyone was dead. Everyone except Wyatt."

Totti knew the first failure might have been forgiven—if Lorenzo even found out about it. But this one would cause problems.

Lorenzo Rossi didn't tolerate failure. Those who let him down were terminated quickly, and without regard. Bodies were rarely, if ever, found.

"Call our contact with the feds," Totti said. "Have him take care of it."

"Shouldn't we call our people in the Miami PD? They were the ones arriving at the scene."

The squad cars had stormed by them only moments before, sirens blaring and lights flashing.

"Our connections with the feds will make sure everyone else falls in line, including our people in Miami PD."

The questions stopped, and for a minute the two rode in silence. They passed a few more first responders—an ambulance and two more cops.

Totti's phone interrupted the quiet. He glanced down at the device resting in the center console wireless charging station, saw Vincenzo Bartolo's name, and picked it up.

"Tell me some good news," Totti said.

"Things that bad in South Florida?"

"They could be better. What's your status?"

Bartolo dragged out his answer for a second. He had a flair for the dramatic, which was a quirk Totti found more annoying than humorous.

"We have Schultz."

The dark temptress of hope caused Totti's heart to skip a beat. No matter how pragmatic, how calculating he was, Totti was still a human—given to the whims of emotion when things seemed at their bleakest turn.

"Excellent," he said, dimming his relief so it didn't show in his voice. "Are you in Orlando?"

"Yes, but we're boarding a plane to New York."

That bit of information didn't have the same effect as the first.

"Why is that?" He tried to mask the suspicion in his tone.

Luciano kept twisting his head slightly to look Totti's way while still trying to keep most of his focus on the road. He couldn't hear what the other guy was saying, and it was obviously driving him mad with curiosity.

"We took his phone from him and unlocked it. His last message was from your guy Sean Wyatt."

"And what did this message say?"

"It seems Wyatt found something in Miami. What it is we don't yet know. But what we do know is that he told Schultz the diamond is hidden in the Richard Morris Hunt Memorial in Central Park."

"Well done, Vincenzo."

"That's not all. Wyatt is on his way to New York now. It seems your operation failed."

Totti's emotions swung to a defensive position. "What's that supposed to mean?"

"How many men did you lose today, Barone? Two? Three? All of them?"

Totti glanced nervously over at the man driving the car. Luciano pretended to be minding his own business.

"That doesn't matter. We got what we needed. That's why I brought you on board with all this, to assure our success. You've done that, my friend. Luciano and I will head to New York immediately. We are on our way to the airport now."

The driver veered onto the ramp leading to the interstate.

"Very well. I trust you've contacted our people to clean up whatever mess you left down there?"

Again, Totti's blood boiled. He almost told Bartolo how he didn't appreciate the other's tone but suppressed his anger enough to only say "I have. It will be taken care of."

"Good. Lorenzo would not be pleased if things were to get more out of hand."

"Things are not out of hand, Vincenzo. Everything is under control. I will personally tell Lorenzo that when I see him."

Bartolo said nothing else. Totti took that to mean he could end the call. "I will see you in New York."

"Okay."

The call ended. Totti looked down at the screen, his nostrils flaring. He continued staring at the device, his mind turning with new plans. He'd known Vincenzo Bartolo a long time. He'd trusted him as much as anyone could be trusted in the world they lived in. But now, Totti wasn't so sure.

There'd been something in the man's voice that betrayed his intentions, and perhaps his ambitions.

The best way to handle a situation such as this was through being proactive. If Totti waited too long to call Rossi, it would make things look worse.

If that were possible.

Totti had just lost seven of Rossi's men. Were they expendable? Sure. Every one of them was, including him and Bartolo. But resources, including men, weren't to be wasted. This would look bad, and only recovering the diamond would change that.

Luciano guided the car along the interstate in silence while Totti thought. The driver held back his instincts to ask what was said on the call, even though the tension he emitted from that desire could have been cut with a chainsaw.

The backup plan had worked. Totti hadn't wanted it to be necessary, but his foresight with this situation had proved correct. Anyone else would have failed entirely. Even though Rossi wouldn't be pleased with the deaths of seven of his men, he would have to applaud Totti's ability to keep control of the situation.

"Where are we going?" Luciano asked, risking Totti's fury.

"New York. Our team in Orlando has a key piece in this game, and we're going to use it to get this Sean Wyatt right where we want him."

Traffic was unusually light on the road to the airport, and the drive took half the time it would have an hour later.

Totti took the silent moment to send a quick text message to the pilot. He'd have to change plans, and that sort of thing didn't happen instantly.

Luciano steered the car off the highway and onto the exit ramp, eventually turning into the airfield, where several private jets sat parked on the tarmac.

Theirs was off to the far right, distanced from the other planes. As they passed through the security gate and drove by a few buildings, Totti noticed a black SUV sitting next to their plane.

He knew the car would be there, waiting for them, along with two more members of the Rossi Clan waiting inside.

They would handle taking this car back, and then further assist in cleaning up the problem at the bookstore—whether it be with bribes or with bullets.

Totti would have preferred it be the former. Bullets were messy. And even when it was dirty, money was the cleaner way to handle things.

Luciano drove the car out to the lonesome spot on the tarmac and then parked the car at an angle so the building behind them was partially blocked from view. The SUV also obstructed the view to the terminal on the other side of the airfield.

When the car stopped, Totti climbed out and slammed the door shut as the two men from the SUV exited their vehicle and came over to meet him.

Luciano stepped out of his side of the car and checked his phone. His face darkened as he read the screen. Maybe he thought Totti wouldn't notice.

Totti narrowed his eyelids as the man's body language changed. Luciano swallowed, sent a quick text, then slid his phone back into his pocket while at the same time drawing a pistol with his other hand.

No one heard the muted pop over the cacophony of jet engines roaring across the airfield. Even if the pistol hadn't been equipped with a suppressor, the sound would have never reached a human ear. Not out here.

The two men who'd been in the SUV stepped over and lifted the body, one on each end, then carried it over to the trunk of the car, loaded it unceremoniously into the cargo bay, and slammed the lid shut.

20

Giulia was stubborn.

Sean had spent five minutes telling the woman there was no way she'd be coming to New York City with him. But she'd insisted. Like a parasite, she wasn't going to leave anytime soon. The search for the diamond was a life's work sort of thing, and while he understood that part of it, Sean had no desire to see her end up dead.

He'd eventually promised her she could come with him to Manhattan but that she would have to stay out of sight once he went to Chelsea Piers. There was no way he'd let her take that risk, even if he had to handcuff her to a desk in a hotel room.

She'd promised to hang back on a barge a few hundred yards from the pier. There was a restaurant and bar there where she could wait until it was all over.

Sean had given her the instructions to remain there, and if she didn't hear from him in the next two hours, to call the cops and report what was going on on the boat.

"Not exactly a boat," Sean muttered as he stood on the docks, staring at a behemoth of a yacht.

He guessed it was 150 feet long, with two stories above the deck and another below. There were a few other luxury yachts parked in slips along the docks, but this one dwarfed them all.

Two men in suits stood on the stern, while more guarded positions in various spots along the deck and on the second-floor balcony.

The white vessel bore only three words for its name—*Fortuna e Potere*. Fortune and Power.

"Subtle."

Two men wearing suits similar to those on the deck approached Sean from the base of the gangway. They wore sunglasses, which seemed a little unnecessary given the fact that it was dark outside.

"Hands up," the guy on Sean's right ordered as they stopped a few feet away. The other guy stepped around behind Sean as he raised his hands and patted him down. He took the book out of Sean's hand, inspected it, and then passed it to the other guy.

"You two ever heard of Corey Hart?" Sean asked as the goon ran his hands around his ankles. Neither answered, probably because they didn't get the joke. "He was a Canadian singer in the '80s. Doesn't ring a bell?"

They said nothing.

"Tough crowd," Sean resigned.

Sean knew he'd be searched, and there wasn't really a good way for him to bring weapons on board the ship.

He'd considered calling in another favor to Emily for assistance, but Sean had put too much on her already in recent days, and requesting backup for something like this wasn't what her agency was designed for. They could handle it, no question, but it was unlikely any of them would be in the area anyway.

The guard finished checking Sean for weapons and then shoved him forward while the other guy made sure no one else was watching. He surveyed the area behind Sean, and then to his left and right before falling in behind the other two.

They ushered Sean up the ramp and onto the deck, where another guard—this one larger than the others, and with a shaved head and black goatee shaped into an upside-down triangle—waited with a grumpy look on his face. It was an expression Sean had seen on a million bar or night club bouncers, one they tried to wear to look tough or threatening.

He turned and opened the door and stepped aside so the three men could enter. Once inside, he closed the door again and resumed his post.

The interior of the ship was spectacular.

Sean had been on a few yachts before, even destroyed one in the Mediterranean off the coast of Corfu. *Good times.* But this one was a floating mansion.

Luxurious white sofas sat to the left next to a wide window that ran from the floor to the ceiling. Opposite those were a few modern club chairs with exposed walnut supports for the armrests and back. The huge windows on both sides gave occupants what had to be a spectacular view on a sunny day at sea.

One of the men shoved Sean in the back toward a corridor through the living room area. He turned and fired the guy a scathing glance, but that was all he could do for the moment. Besides, even if he tried to take out these guys, the head of the snake was still somewhere on board.

He passed through a spot in the hall that narrowed slightly then opened up again into a massive dining room. The table was made of pale wood, which also adorned sections of the walls to offset the white marble floor tiles underfoot.

A man sat at the head of the table with his hands folded atop it. His hair was salt and pepper, and he had a perfectly sculpted beard to match. Dark circles surrounded the man's blue eyes. His jaw was narrow but strong. He wore a gray suit that cost more than most people made in a month.

Sean guessed Armani.

"Ah," the man said. "You must be the illustrious Sean Wyatt. Please, come in. Sit." He motioned to a chair opposite Tommy, who sat in a seat next to him. Two muscular guards stood behind Tommy. Another man, who looked to be in his early fifties, stood off to the side near the man in charge.

"I am Franco Rossi," the boss said. "I'm so glad you decided to join us."

"Went and got yourself caught again, eh, Schultzie?" Sean joked, ignoring Rossi.

"Uber driver. How was I supposed to know?"

"Bloody rideshares."

"I'm sure this little reunion would be full of delightful banter were we to continue," Rossi said, "but we must, regrettably, get down to business."

The guy sounded Italian, just like all the others. His voice was commanding, though Sean couldn't figure out his relation to *the* Lorenzo Rossi.

"Where's Lorenzo?" Sean asked pointedly. "I've heard of him. You, well, I haven't."

"Yes. That's not surprising. Lorenzo is my older brother. I oversee our interests here in New York." He spoke with the confidence of a guy who didn't believe he could lose. At anything in life.

The guard carrying the book walked over to the man and handed it to him.

"This is what you found in Miami?" the boss asked, pulling the tome over so it was in front of his chest. He tapped on the cover.

"Yeah. Just before I iced four of your goons. You really should have better hiring practices."

The insult visibly irritated the man, but only for a second. Then it rolled off his shoulders, and he opened the book to look inside.

"Curious inscription," he said. "My associate here tells me you believe the diamond is located at the Richard Hunt Memorial in Central Park."

Sean shrugged. "Maybe. Maybe it's at the bottom of the Atlantic Ocean. No one really knows for sure."

The boss smiled and flipped the page to the picture of the memorial. "Ah, I see now why you think it's here." He obviously didn't buy Sean's weak attempt at suggesting the gem was on the ocean floor. "First, the trail leads to Buenos Aires, a known destination for the diamond after it was purchased from the former emperor. Then it takes you to Miami, another place the legend of the diamond suggests. I didn't expect New York City to be the location where we would find it."

"Were you thinking of somewhere else?" Tommy asked. "Because as my friend here just told you, it could be anywhere."

The man chuckled at his prisoner's desperation. "No, I think your friend has figured it out. That is, after all, what you two are good at. Haven't you, Sean?"

Sean cleared his throat. "Yes. The diamond is hidden in the memorial."

"See?" Rossi said to Tommy. "This is good. The truth shall set you free, as they say."

"What's your idea of free?" Sean groused. He asked the question, but he knew how men like this thought. They were killers, and the only way Tommy and Sean were going to be free was when they—or these goons—were dead at the bottom of the Hudson River.

"So, how does it work?" Rossi asked.

Sean and Tommy shared a questioning glance.

"What do you mean?" Sean asked, bringing his eyes back to the man in charge. "How does what work?"

"Well, the diamond must be in some kind of hiding place. A vault, a chest, a safe. Is it buried under the monument?"

Sean didn't know, and he was well aware that if he hesitated even for a second, Rossi would know the truth.

A door burst open from the back of the boat. The sound startled everyone in the room and caused the guard behind Sean and the two behind Tommy to draw the firearms from within their jackets and point them toward the corridor.

A man walked in that Sean didn't recognize. He was dressed more casually than the henchmen but not as lavishly as Rossi. It was more like crime business casual.

Sean noticed a surprised look on the man's face standing next to Rossi.

"Oh, hello, everyone. Glad to see you've already started."

"Barone," Rossi said, standing with arms spread in a welcoming gesture. "Vincenzo here said you weren't going to make it. That you were stuck in Miami."

"Oh, I'm sure he did," the one named Barone replied. There was something in his tone, a malevolence that hinted to deep-seated animosity—and most likely a high propensity toward violence. Sean figured this guy ran the muscle for the organization.

Vincenzo looked as if he'd seen a ghost.

"Barone. I'm glad you're here," the man stammered.

Barone shook his head as he approached then drew a pistol out of his jacket. He pointed the weapon at Vincenzo, aiming just past Sean's head.

"Whoa. What are you doing?" Rossi demanded. "Put that away, Barone." He stood and extended a finger at him. "We're all on the same side here."

"Are we, Franco? Are we?" Barone's eyes were wild, like a rabid animal full of insanity fueled by bloodlust.

"He ordered a hit on me," Barone snarled. "You think I'm stupid, Vincenzo? I know you told Luciano to kill me. You tried to get me out of the way so you could take my place. Convenient that you're standing there by Franco's side. Right where you want to be in the grand scheme of things."

Fear streaked Vincenzo's eyes as his face blanched further.

Sean and Tommy watched the unexpected turn of events unfold. And both of them paid close attention to the guards with the guns. Sean had wondered if and when he'd have an opportunity to make a move. He hadn't thought it would come so soon, or in such an unusual way.

"Put the gun down, Barone," Franco ordered. His voice was stern, and his face was dark with anger. He'd had enough of whatever this was.

Barone reached into his right-front pocket while keeping his weapon trained on Vincenzo. He pulled out a phone, set it on the table, and slid it over to the boss.

The man stopped it before it fell off the edge, slapping his palm down on it. "What is this?" Franco asked.

"Luciano's phone. Read the last message."

The boss questioned the command with a silent glower, but he picked it up anyway and checked the screen.

He read the message and then looked over at Vincenzo, the questions in his eyes quickly turning to accusation.

"What is the meaning of this?"

"Franco," Vincenzo started. "I—"

"Don't lie to me," the boss raged. "I give the orders for who lives and dies here. Not you. You have betrayed your brother, and without authorization."

Franco reached into his suit jacket and drew a shiny silver pistol. The gaudy weapon looked more like a showpiece than a functional firearm. The barrel was wrapped with an engraved black serpent whose head ended at the muzzle; maw opened wide with fangs protruding from the roof of its mouth.

It was a little over the top, but Sean had to admit the gun's appearance was cool, like something out of a movie.

"Franco," Vincenzo pleaded. "His recklessness cost you seven men. I had to clean up his mess. Three dead in Argentina. And four in Miami. All his fault. If I hadn't stepped in and taken over, you wouldn't have that book, or these two."

The boss's expression changed again. He looked more confused than angry now, but a sense of betrayal pulled on his cheekbones like gravity itself had doubled.

"Is this true, Barone? You lost seven men, and you didn't tell me or Lorenzo?"

Now it was Barone's turn to feel the heat.

Sean noticed that none of the guards were paying him or Tommy any attention now. They were caught in a tennis match, their heads going back and forth, uncertain which side they were supposed to take. Their boss, too, appeared to be calculating who he could trust in all this.

As Barone was formulating an answer, something Sean figured would be quite the story, someone else spoke for him from just beyond the corner of the hallway.

"It is true," a woman said.

A second later, Giulia appeared behind Barone. Her right elbow was tucked close to her side. She held a pistol with a suppressor on the end in her hand.

In that instant, any hope Sean had of getting out of this alive evaporated.

21

Sean and Tommy's eyes met. They shared an unspoken "wow" at the sudden twist. Neither of them had seen this coming, but they both knew drawing attention to themselves right now by simply uttering a word was not the prudent thing to do.

The only chance they had of survival was some sort of Mexican standoff where everyone else in the room killed each other.

"Giulia," Franco said. "What a pleasant surprise."

"I hope you weren't going to fire that thing," she said, nodding at the pistol in his hand. "We'd all be deaf for days."

The man's eyes wandered to the decorative pistol, then he shrugged with a grin like a boy who'd been caught stealing cookies from a jar.

"I suppose you're right," he allowed and lowered the weapon.

"Barone's recklessness cost you men," she said. "And I hardly think Vincenzo's motives were pure in trying to handle the situation."

"You watch your tongue—"

"How dare you speak to me," she growled, raising the pistol. "Know your place, boy."

Franco remained oddly silent, and it made Sean wonder who she really was, and what her role could be in the Rossi organization.

He was still trying to understand how he'd missed the signals—if there had been any. She'd played the part of a weak damsel to the letter. Her credentials had checked out, too, which wasn't something a novice could simply slip by someone like Sean. Whatever game she was up to had to be a long play, one that had been years in the making.

The guards watched on, visibly mesmerized by the drama. They looked almost paralyzed by it, and none of them seemed to be ready to do anything, much less take a side.

This was not lost on Sean, and he calculated what possible action he could take to get out of this mess.

"Franco," Barone barked. "Yes, I lost seven men. But my plan still worked. It was I who brought Vincenzo in to assist in bringing these two to you. If not for me, none of this would be possible. You must ask yourself who you can trust now. Me, the one who brought you the diamond, or him, an ambitious man willing to do whatever it takes to climb the ladder. I have always been loyal to you."

"How dare you!" Vincenzo spat. "You piece of—"

"Let me kill him," Barone interrupted. "He deserves it."

Franco thought for a long, painful moment. Then he turned to the guard behind Tommy's left shoulder and motioned him to come forward.

The man obeyed and moved next to his boss. Franco held out his palm, and the guard drew a small pistol from his jacket—this one with a suppressor on it. He placed it in Franco's hand and retreated back a step.

The leader looked down at the weapon, then curled his fingers around it and pointed it at Vincenzo. "I can't have traitors in my midst," he said.

"No," Vincenzo begged. "Listen to reason. I have never—"

The muzzle puffed with a click. The round disappeared into Vincenzo's chest, leaving a hole where it entered. The man looked down at the wound, horror filling his eyes. Then he lifted his gaze to meet Franco's.

The boss aimed higher and fired one more shot into the man's head.

He fell against the wall, hitting it with the back of his bloody skull, and drooped to the floor.

"Thank you, sir" Barone said, lowering his weapon slightly. "You made the—"

Franco swiveled and fired again, this time at Barone. The bullet found his gut.

As he grimaced in agony, he tried to raise the pistol to defend himself, but Giulia fired into the back of the man's head, dropping him to the floor near the table.

The kill shot surprised Sean and Tommy. Even though she'd brandished the weapon like someone ready to do the deed, neither of them had expected her to actually use it.

"Now," she said, lowering the pistol back to her side, the muzzle pointing at the floor, let's get down to business, shall we?"

Franco appeared pleased at her businesslike approach.

Hazy smoke lingered in the room, and it swirled around her as she walked toward the head of the table.

"Get rid of them," Franco said to the guard behind Tommy's right shoulder.

The muscular man nodded once and stepped around the table to where Barone's body lay. He grabbed the ankles and dragged the dead man out through the narrow corridor toward the living room.

"This is going to be a mess to clean up," Franco realized, noting the blood on the walls and on the floor.

"Indeed," Giulia said. She glanced at Sean, who only allowed a stoic glare. He wouldn't give her the satisfaction of begging, not from his words or his body language.

"Did these two tell you how to access the diamond?" she asked.

"Not yet. We were just getting to that."

Sean noticed Giulia standing just behind Franco, the pistol drifting toward the base of his neck.

"Things are never quite what they seem," Giulia said, flashing her eyes toward Sean. "We must always be ready for the unexpected in matters such as this."

Sean narrowed his eyelids at the comment. Then he realized what was about to happen.

The suppressor muzzle pressed against Franco's skull as she leaned forward.

"What are you doing?" Rossi asked. He sounded as if he wasn't sure she was joking around.

The two remaining guards realized what she was doing, but one was unarmed, and the other was uncertain. The latter reached into his jacket, but she shook her head and made a clicking sound with her tongue.

"Don't," she cautioned.

The guard froze.

"What is this?" Franco demanded. "Don't point that at me. Have you gone mad?"

"Do you know what will drive a person mad?" Giulia asked. "Watching your brother, Lorenzo, murder my family for information about the Florentine Diamond's whereabouts. Watching him torture my father before putting a bullet through his head. I was there that day he and his thugs killed them. All I could do was hide in the closet, too scared to move or say anything."

Sean saw the man's eyes widen with fear, though there was still confusion lingering within the pupils.

"My family are the descendants of the diamond's cutter. Lorenzo thought we knew where it was. And he would stop at nothing to find it. And for what? To prove himself to your family?"

"I don't know what you're talking about," Franco blurted.

"Perhaps. Or perhaps you're lying. I don't care either way. You're going to die. And when I'm done with you, I will find your brother, and I will bring your family's reign to an end."

Grim reality chiseled Franco's face. "If you murder me, you will not get off this boat alive. My men will kill you before you can touch the ramp."

"I guess we will just have to take that risk," she said.

"No. Wait."

The pistol clicked. Red mist spewed out of his right cheek just below the eye.

The two guards jumped, startled by the abrupt execution.

Sean kicked his chair back and drove it into the guy behind him as the man tried to draw his weapon. The chair pinned the goon against the wall long enough for Sean to stand, turn, and drive his fist squarely across the man's jaw. Bone cracked as the guy's head snapped to the right. Sean didn't let up and grabbed the side of his skull with both hands and smashed it into the wall three times until the man's legs went limp and he fell to the floor unconscious.

At the same time, Tommy spun out of his chair and whipped his elbow around his guard's temple. The shot to the head dropped the man instantly, knocking him out cold.

Both the Americans immediately set to checking the unconscious guards for additional weapons but found none.

"Here," Giulia said, sliding the one Rossi held over to Tommy.

"Thanks." He grabbed the gun as Sean stood upright, now equipped with the pistol he'd taken from his guard.

There was no time for planning their escape. Two men with similar weapons stood just beyond a huge window behind Giulia, aiming through the glass.

"Get down!" Sean ordered.

Giulia looked back over her shoulder and then dove toward Sean as he and Tommy squeezed their triggers.

Their muzzles erupted, bullets puncturing the sheet of glass and burrowing into the guards on the deck beyond.

The gunmen flailed as the bullets riddled their torsos, and then they fell to the wood at their feet.

Sean turned at a sound behind him and fired another shot as the guard who'd dragged out Barone's body returned around the corner.

The man never had a chance, catching a round in the upper chest and another in the head.

"Come on," Sean said to the others. "Giulia, stay behind me. Tommy, cover the rear."

"On it," Tommy said as he shifted over to help Giulia off the floor. "You really had me going for a minute there."

"Sorry for the ruse," she replied. "I've been after the Rossi brothers for a long time."

"So this was never about the diamond?" Tommy asked.

"Not the time, Schultzie," Sean said, pushing forward slowly, crossing one foot in front of the other toward the door.

"Right. Sorry. Later."

Giulia fell in line behind Sean and followed him, stepping carefully around the smeared blood on the white floor, until they reached the open door.

Sean leaned into the left side of the door and aimed his pistol through the opening. The guard standing there turned his head in time to see the flash of the muzzle.

Giulia tucked in behind Sean, and Tommy took a position on the other side of the door, peeking out at the opposite angle to make sure the way was clear.

"What about the men on the second deck?" he whispered, pointing up.

"I'll handle them," Sean said. "Tommy, you check below and make sure there aren't any others. Giulia stay here, and get ready to run for it."

"What?"

Sean passed her a look that demanded obedience.

"Okay, fine. But don't get yourself killed trying to be a hero."

"Haven't died yet," Sean quipped and took off toward a set of stairs in the rear of the room.

He silently climbed the steps, pointing the pistol up into the stairwell as he moved. At the top, he heard footsteps. They were moving in a hurry, and Sean knew why. Someone had raised the alarm. Maybe they'd seen the two men gunned down on the bow, or perhaps one of the guards had called in the trouble inside the dining room just before getting taken out. Either way, the noises from above indicated more trouble.

The first gunman appeared at the top of the steps. He was rushing, unaware that there was anyone in the stairwell. His recklessness earned him a round to the gut and one in the face, along with a tumble down the stairs.

Sean avoided the body as it rolled by him and focused upward as he kept moving.

He reached the top of the stairs, and the door to the left burst open. Another gunman appeared in the doorway, and Sean fired a round that hit the man in the left shoulder. The guard twisted from the impact, but managed to raise his pistol and get off a shot that sent Sean diving for cover behind a couch with a zebra-print blanket over it.

A television in the corner reflected the man's movement at the door. Sean saw it, moved forward, and then popped up to fire another round, this time hitting the man squarely in the center of the chest.

The gunman staggered backward one step before Sean sent the kill shot through his neck.

He tumbled down the stairs toward the other dead guy, leaving Sean alone in the entertainment room. A luxurious bar with literal top-shelf liquor stood across from him. Sean kept his weapon aimed at the open doorway, waiting, but no one else came through.

After giving it nearly a minute, he rushed over, leaned against the wall, and peered out. He didn't see anyone else, but that didn't mean he and the others were in the clear.

He switched sides, looked out the other direction, and then made his move onto the walkway. The cold December air chilled his skin. His breath plumed out of his mouth in smoky clouds.

At the corner, he paused. A shadow slipped across the deck in front of him. He waited, then spun and squeezed the trigger as the sights fell on a gunman moving toward him.

The pistol didn't fire.

Sean thought he'd counted every round but must have lost track. The guard pointed his weapon, but Sean grabbed the barrel, twisted it, and heard a crack in the man's hand. The guy yelped, but the cry of pain cut short as Sean drove his right elbow into his throat, crushing the windpipe.

He doubled over, and Sean helped him by pushing down on the back of the man's head while driving his knee up. The kneecap plowed straight into the thug's nose with a nauseating crunch.

The gunman's grip on the pistol failed, and Sean turned it on him and finished the job with a single shot through the right temple.

His pulse raced as he circled around the next corner of the deck, but he saw no other men waiting.

Sean took a full lap around the ship until he'd cleared the deck, then entered into the wheelhouse to make sure everyone was taken care of.

He found the ship's captain sitting in a high-back leather chair in front of three state-of-the-art monitors and the controls to the yacht.

The man was drinking a cup of coffee, listening to something on a pair of noise-canceling headphones. He never knew Sean was there.

Sean backed out of the control room and returned down the stairs.

He found Tommy and Giulia waiting by the door where he'd left them.

"Anyone below deck?" Sean asked.

Tommy shook his head. "Not that I saw. But I barricaded the door so if anyone was hiding, they won't be getting out anytime soon."

"Good enough. I say we get out of here."

Sean looked out to the docks and again down both sides of the ship before leading the other two along the deck and over to the ramp. He allowed Tommy and Giulia to pass, then followed them down to shore while covering the rear. Once on the docks again, he tossed the pistol into the murky black water and walked quickly away toward the streets beyond the buildings of Chelsea Piers.

As they hurried through the cold, dark New York night, Sean looked back a dozen times to make sure they weren't being followed. But he never saw any figures emerge from the shadows.

They reached the street, and Tommy stuck out his hand to hail a cab. After a few tries, one of the cars pulled over to the curb. Tommy opened the door for Giulia, then went around to the other side.

She and Sean climbed in, and the driver asked where they were headed.

"Central Park," Tommy answered.

"No," Sean corrected. "We're going to LaGuardia."

Tommy and Giulia both turned their heads and faced him with confusion dripping from their eyes.

"What?" Tommy asked.

"LaGuardia. We're not going to the park."

"You guys sound like you can't make up your minds," the driver said, sounding a little irritated and entertained.

Tommy saw the look in his friend's eyes, and surrendered. "Okay, fine. Airport it is. But I would love to hear this one."

The driver pulled away from the curb after flipping on the fare. The city lights passed by through the window against the backdrop of a bright winter moon.

"You going to tell us what's going on?" Tommy asked when they were five minutes away from the piers.

Sean nodded. "What we're looking for isn't at the monument in Central Park."

"How do you know that?" Giulia wondered.

"Yeah, I mean, you came all the way to New York to find it," Tommy added.

"I came to New York because you got nicked by the Rossis. But I didn't know the—" he stopped himself, thinking it better to not say the word *diamond* within earshot of the driver. "I didn't know it wasn't here until Rossi was talking about where it could be hidden. I got to thinking. It doesn't make sense that the thing would be in such a public place, with no security. And then it hit me."

He paused and waited.

"What hit you?" Tommy insisted.

"Richard Hunt was a famous architect. And one of the most impressive of all the properties he designed is also one with a significant collection of pieces from Italy." They kept their eyes squarely locked on him in anticipation. "This property was owned by a family who had a keen interest in the preservation of Italian design and architecture. So much so, they brought one peculiar piece to the grounds and installed it there in a courtyard. It's called the Hunt Fountain, but it came from Italy. And it's on the grounds of the Biltmore Estate in North Carolina."

22

ASHEVILLE, NORTH CAROLINA

The magnificent Biltmore Estate glowed like a palatial stone Christmas tree. The glittering lights radiated into the cold mountain air to the point they dimmed the stars in the heavens above.

Sean stood by his wife, Adriana, holding her hand as they gazed upon the wondrous sight. Tommy and his wife, June, stood next to them, with Giulia in the middle of the four.

They surrounded a stone fountain in a quiet and largely ignored-by-the-public courtyard of the Biltmore Estate.

Christmas was only a few days away, and most of the grounds were packed with tourists there to see one of the most impressive displays of holiday decorations and lights anywhere in the world.

Tickets were always sold out for this time of year, but Tommy had pulled some strings with a friend based in nearby Fletcher.

They'd spent an hour walking the grounds and touring the mansion before finding their way here, to the Hunt Fountain—an octagonal Italian Renaissance piece with reliefs of men's heads and torsos gazing out from each corner, along with other seemingly random designs of horned creatures, flowers, and coats of arms.

The air was cold and fresh, with hints of evergreen and dried leaves laced on the breeze from the surrounding forests.

"You really think it's in there?" Giulia asked, staring at the stone fountain.

Water spewed from an umbrella-shaped spigot in the center and splashed into the pool within the basin.

Sean rolled his head around to loosen his neck. "Yeah. I do."

Tommy huffed. "I mean, we'll never really know, will we? It could be at the memorial monument in Central Park."

"No," Sean said. "It's here. Where it can be protected. That was the family's intention all along. To keep it safe, as they did for so much Italian and other European culture through the years."

Giulia sighed. "It would have been nice to actually see it, though."

No one said anything for a couple of minutes.

"What are you going to do?" Sean asked. "Head back to Italy and your agency? Or was that just a ruse?"

Giulia laughed. "No, I really am an archaeologist. And yes, I will return to my post. But I'm not done with the Rossis. They have to pay for what they've done. Sooner or later, Lorenzo will slip up, and I will get to him."

"Sounds like a dangerous proposition, from what I understand," June said, chiming in.

"If you would like some help," Adriana entered, "and I'm in the area, let me know."

"Thank you. All of you. You've done more than I could have ever asked for. And I have closure to a chapter of my life that desperately needed it. But if things get to that point, I will reach out. For now, I just want to take in this moment. We are standing in the presence of an artifact that no one has seen for over a hundred years, was held by the hands of emperors and kings, and sought after for centuries."

"Pretty crazy when you think about it," Sean quipped.

"Yes," she agreed. "It certainly is."

THANK YOU

As always, I hope you enjoyed this story.

The case of the missing Florentine Diamond is a fascinating one, and one that has yet to be solved—at least as far as public knowledge is concerned.

I built this story around speculation of where the diamond went after it left the possession of the emperor, though no one really knows the truth.

The Vanderbilt family did have a keen interest in European, and especially Italian culture, art, architecture, and cuisine. Some of the descendants of Commodore Vanderbilt actually moved to Europe to be immersed in those facets of life.

If you have never had the chance to visit the Biltmore Estate in Asheville, North Carolina, I highly recommend it. The property is one of the most spectacular pieces of real estate in the United States.

Asheville, too, is a beautiful city, nestled in the Appalachian Mountains of Western North Carolina. With more than forty breweries, a delightful food culture, and intriguing architecture throughout downtown, I'm sure you'll find something to enjoy, and perhaps a new mystery or two.

Thanks so much for joining me, Sean, Tommy, and Adriana on this adventure.

I'll see you in the next one.

Your friendly neighborhood author,

Ernest

ALSO BY ERNEST DEMPSEY

Sean Wyatt Adventures:

The Secret of the Stones

The Cleric's Vault

The Last Chamber

The Grecian Manifesto

The Norse Directive

Game of Shadows

The Jerusalem Creed

The Samurai Cipher

The Cairo Vendetta

The Uluru Code

The Excalibur Key

The Denali Deception

The Sahara Legacy

The Fourth Prophecy

The Templar Curse

The Forbidden Temple

The Omega Project

The Napoleon Affair

The Second Sign

The Milestone Protocol

Where Horizons End

Poseidon's Fury

Adriana Villa Adventures:

War of Thieves Box Set

When Shadows Call

Shadows Rising

Shadow Hour

The Adventure Guild (ALL AGES):

The Caesar Secret: Books 1-3

The Carolina Caper

Beta Force:

Operation Zulu

London Calling

Paranormal Archaeology Division:

Hell's Gate

Guardians of Earth:

Emergence: Gideon Wolf Book 1

Righteous Dawn: Gideon Wolf Book 2

Crimson Winter: Gideon Wolf Book 3

The Relic Runner - A Dak Harper Series:

The Relic Runner Origin Story

The Courier

Two Nights In Mumbai

Country Roads

Heavy Lies the Crown

Moscow Sky

Thief's Honor

ACKNOWLEDGMENTS

As always, I would like to thank my terrific editors, Anne and Jason, for their hard work. What they do makes my stories so much better for readers all over the world. Anne Storer and Jason Whited are the best editorial team a writer could hope for and I appreciate everything they do.

I also want to thank Elena at Li Graphics for her tremendous work on my book covers and for always overdelivering. Elena rocks.

A big thank you has to go out to my friend James Slater for his proofing work. James has added another layer of quality control to these stories, and I can't thank him enough.

Last but not least, I need to thank all my wonderful fans and especially the advance reader team. Their feedback and reviews are always so helpful and I can't say enough good things about all of them.